Matthew Reilly is the internationally bestselling author of the *Scarecrow* novels: *Ice Station, Area 7, Scarecrow, Scarecrow and the Army of Thieves* and the novella *Hell Island*; the *Jack West* novels: *Seven Ancient Wonders, The Six Sacred Stones, The Five Greatest Warriors* and *The Four Legendary Kingdoms*; and the stand-alone novels *Contest, Temple, Hover Car Racer, The Tournament* and *The Great Zoo of China*.

His books are published in over 20 languages, with worldwide sales of over 7 million copies.

Also by Matthew Reilly

MATTHEW REILLY

TROLL MOUNTAIN

PAN

Pan Macmillan Australia

This is a work of fiction. Characters, institutions and organisations mentioned in this novel are either the product of the author's imagination or, if real, used fictitiously without any intent to describe actual conduct.

First published 2014 in Momentum by Pan Macmillan Australia Pty Ltd
This Pan edition published 2016 by Pan Macmillan Australia Pty Ltd
1 Market Street, Sydney, New South Wales, Australia, 2000

Copyright © Karanadon Entertainment Pty Limited 2014

The moral right of the author has been asserted.

All rights reserved. No part of this book may be reproduced or transmitted by any person or entity (including Google, Amazon or similar organisations), in any form or by any means, electronic or mechanical, including photocopying, recording, scanning or by any information storage and retrieval system, without prior permission in writing from the publisher.

Cataloguing-in-Publication entry is available
from the National Library of Australia
http://catalogue.nla.gov.au

Typeset in 12/18 pt Sabon by Post Pre-press Group
Printed by IVE

MIX
Paper | Supporting
responsible forestry
FSC
www.fsc.org
FSC® C018183

TROLL
MOUNTAIN

Exactly where the notion of a large, thick-skinned, semi-intelligent and usually hostile creature known as a troll originated is not known.

Some anthropologists have postulated that the term 'troll' was used by early humans to describe isolated groups of declining hominids: Neanderthals, Cro-Magnons, or even the so-called 'Missing Link' in the human evolutionary chain. Others suggest that trolls were simply another species of mega-fauna—like mammoths and sabre-toothed cats—that became extinct as northern climates warmed . . .

FROM: *THE ORIGINS OF MYTHOLOGY*

DOUGLAS MACKENZIE

W.M. LAWRY & CO., LONDON, 1974

**MANY YEARS AGO
IN A LAND FAR TO THE NORTH ...**

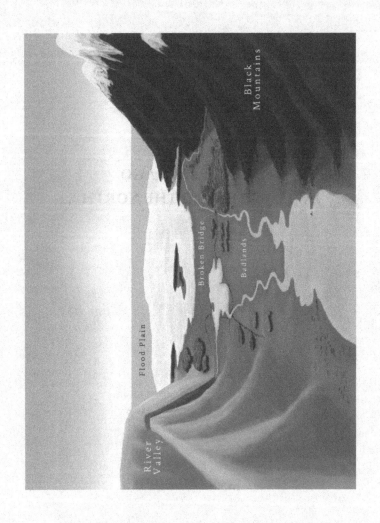

THE VALLEY AND SURROUNDS

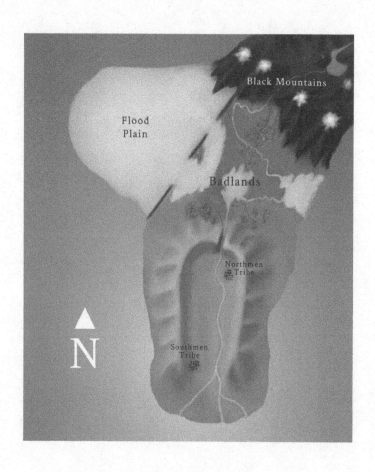

THE VALLEY AND SURROUNDS

O nce upon a time in a river valley far to the north, there lived a tribe whose members suddenly started dying from a mysterious illness.

It was a singularly horrible way to die. Pus-filled sores would appear on the victim's skin, then their gums would begin to bleed. Soon, unable to move, covered in boils and with their teeth falling out, the victim would fall asleep, never to wake.

Then, as if to compound the tribe's misery, the river that flowed into their valley from the north dried up.

Even though the tribe had sent forth its annual tribute to the trolls, the trolls had decided to cut the flow of water from their dam upstream. This was something the trolls did from time to time, for no other reason, it seemed, than to remind those who lived in the valley of the trolls' cruel dominance over them.

In a few short months the lands in and around the valley became dry and barren. The soil crumbled. Game became scarce. It was said that even the hobgoblins—who with their wiry little bodies could survive for longer in tougher conditions than just about any other creature—had abandoned their lair in the low mountains in search of more plentiful lands.

For the Northmen tribe, things became parlous. The harvest was so poor that food was rationed. And it soon became apparent that the lack of both food and water was aiding the spread of the illness. Tribe members fell ill in greater numbers.

Prayers were offered to the gods. They did no good.

Sacred essences were burned. That also did no good.

More members of the tribe were struck down by the disease.

Something had to be done.

Two elders were dispatched to begin talks with the trolls, to beseech them to release more water. They departed wearing their best robes and the distinctive wooden necklaces worn only by elders.

Those elders never returned.

*

Then came worse news.

It became known that the trolls themselves were also suffering from the terrible illness but that they had chanced upon a cure for it, an elixir of some sort. It was further said that upon payment of a 'special tribute' the trolls promised to cure any tribe's victims of the disease.

Some leaders of the smaller tribes in the valley had gone to Troll Mountain with their sick to enter into this pact with the Troll King and, at the same time, to beg him to release more water.

A week later, the sick returned to the river valley, miraculously cured of the disease, with tales of drinking the fabled Elixir—a stinging yellow liquid.

Unfortunately, they reported that the Troll King had flatly refused to release any extra water from his dam, keeping the tribes of the river valley firmly under his thumb.

More ominously, the tribal *leaders* who had conveyed their sick to Troll Mountain did *not* return.

The cured had no knowledge of what had happened to their leaders in the Mountain King's halls, but deep in their hearts they all had the same suspicions.

*

Such was the life of the people of the Northmen tribe.

After a time, however, it was noticed by some that while the river dried up and the crops failed and the Northmen fell ill in greater numbers, the head family continued to eat well.

For generations, the chieftain's family had been taller than the other members of the tribe, sturdier, stronger, and so they designated themselves the tribe's warriors. And since it was imperative that they remain healthy so they could defend their people from the other major tribe in the valley, the Southmen, the head family got first rights to the already limited supply of food—and only then, of course, after tribute had been sent to the trolls.

'They are only the warriors because they keep the art of wielding weapons within their own family,' Raf grumbled to his sister, Kira, as they left the chief's elongated hut one day, having just delivered to the head family an extra share of their meagre harvest.

'Quiet, Raf,' Kira whispered. 'You'll get into trouble again.'

'And the more they eat, the stronger they remain, so they perpetuate their high status—'

'Shh!'

'What can they do to me?' Raf said.

'They can banish you.'

'The way things are, banishment is hardly much of a punishment. What difference is it to anyone if I starve here or elsewhere?'

'It would make a difference to me,' Kira said softly, touching his arm. Their parents had died when they were young. Kira shrugged. 'It is how things are, and how they have always been. The big have their way. The small, like us, survive.'

Raf frowned. 'I don't like the way things are. They could be better.'

*

But the truth was, Raf *was* small and had always been so. Even though he had just reached his seventeenth year, he was boyish in appearance, thin and gangly, with a mop of unruly sandy hair.

However, what he lacked in strength, he made up for in speed: he was nimble and fast, which in his younger days had helped him avoid a thrashing or two at the hands of bigger boys. And he was an exceptional climber—of trees and high rocks—which had also helped him dodge a few beatings.

It should also be mentioned that Raf was inventive. He spent all his spare moments designing new farming implements, cooking utensils and some-times—in defiance of the tribe's rules—weapons.

The invention that Raf looked upon with particular pride was his rope: an ultra-long spool that he himself had braided together over many months. Fully extended, it was perhaps fifty feet long. And it was strong. It had to be, since Raf used it to scale the cliffs at the rim of the valley, hundreds of feet above a sheer drop.

His mother had actively encouraged his inventiveness. Serene and calm, she would examine each of Raf's new inventions and ask him pointed questions, sometimes causing him to dash off to make amendments to his original designs. But when the item was finished, she would always use it, which made the young Raf especially proud.

Sadly, encouragement of this kind was not common in Raf's tribe.

Once, as a boy, Raf had offered to help the chief build weapons for the tribe's warriors. He'd even made a special sample to show the chief: a double-bladed axe. Till then, the tribe had only used axes with a single blade.

The fat chief had roared with laughter, saying in a booming voice, 'What fool would use a double-bladed axe in battle? I only need one blade to bring down my enemies! Leave the fighting to us, boy!'

The other members of the head family had guffawed, especially Bader, the chief's third son who, although the same age as Raf and once his childhood playmate, now stood a foot taller than Raf and ordered Raf around as if he were an elder.

Raf had left the chief's hut embarrassed and humiliated.

In a tribe based around families and a ruling clan, it didn't help that Raf and his sister were orphans.

It had happened when Raf was twelve and Kira eight.

One day their mother had not returned from gathering berries in the hills with the other women. Instead, one of the women had raced into the village, screaming: 'Troll! Rogue troll!'

Their father had immediately dashed off toward the berry hills, followed by a group of warriors (who, Raf thought, hadn't moved quickly enough).

Leaving Kira with a neighbour, Raf had hurried after them, tracking them first by the sound of their voices and then by their footprints.

As he arrived at the berry hill on the eastern rim of the valley, he heard the troll.

A deep guttural roar echoed through the trees, followed by shouts, the crash of branches and the *swoosh* of a giant hammer being swung.

'Force it back! Force it back against the cliff!'

Raf arrived at a spot where the top of the berry hill met the base of a high rocky wall. There he was stopped by one of the younger warriors.

'Raf!' the youth said. 'Don't go any further! You shouldn't see—'

But Raf had to see.

He pushed past the young warrior and burst out into the clearing to behold—

—a great troll gripping his mother like a rag doll and bellowing at the five adult warriors surrounding it and prodding it with spears.

The great grey creature was only a couple of handspans taller than a man, just shy of seven feet, but it was far bulkier than any man Raf had ever seen: it had broad shoulders, a thick neck, and a brutish block of a head that was all forehead and jaw. Its skin was a thick hide like that of an elephant.

The troll stood with its back to the rock wall, trapped, holding Raf's mother around the waist in one of its mighty hands while with the other it lashed out with a huge battle hammer.

In horror, Raf saw that his mother's eyes were closed and that her body swayed lifelessly with every movement the troll made. His mother, his beautiful, calm and encouraging mother.

His father rushed forward to grab her hand.

'No—!' someone yelled, but it was too late. The troll swung its massive hammer round and it struck Raf's father square in the head, sending him slamming into the rock wall. He hit the wall with terrible force and crumpled, killed in an instant.

Raf screamed in horror.

Then, with another bellowing roar the troll discarded its hammer, threw Raf's mother over its shoulder and clambered up the rock wall, out of sight.

Raf never saw his mother again.

*

As he grew into his teens, Raf kept more and more to himself.

His sister Kira worried about him, doted on him, and often shushed him when he voiced his increasingly dissatisfied views of the head family. He had felt the warriors' efforts to save his mother had been half-hearted, ineffective, and hadn't justified their extra allotment of food.

Which was why, when he wasn't farming his little plot with Kira or constructing implements that made their toil a little easier, in secret he would practise with his weapons.

He made his double-bladed axe smaller and lighter so that it could be wielded with greater speed. He even gave this new model a hollow handle, inside of which he slid a long, thin knife made of flint.

When he went hunting at the edge of the Badlands, which lay to the north of the river valley, Raf would practise extracting the knife from the axe's handle, executing the move very quickly so that if he were ever confronted by an enemy, he would have weapons in both hands in the blink of an eye. He practised thrusting and slashing with his weapons in a dance-like motion. Had anyone been watching him, Raf thought, they surely would have thought him mad.

As it turned out, unbeknownst to Raf, there

was often someone watching him as he practised alone by the edge of the Badlands.

At the height of his disgruntlement, during one year's summer harvest festivities, Raf did an outrageous thing: he asked to compete in the annual harvest games.

During the harvest, the ruling family always held games. These usually involved fights and wrestling matches between the chieftain's sons, allowing them to show off their warrior skills. Even in lean times, the games were very popular among the tribesfolk.

When Raf asked to compete in a wrestling match, the fat chief laughed loudly, just as he had done before—but this time Raf asked him in front of the tribe and all were watching the exchange closely.

The chief threw a look to his sons before nodding nonchalantly. 'Are you certain you want to do this, lad? Farm boys should not challenge warriors. I would not like to see you get hurt.'

Some of the tribesfolk tittered.

'I would still like to try,' Raf said.

The chieftain shook his head and said to the crowd, 'Let no one say I didn't warn him!' He turned back to Raf. 'Fine. You shall wrestle Bader then.'

His heart pounding, Raf stepped into the makeshift dirt ring and faced off against Bader. As the fight began, they circled each other, and then Raf pushed off the ground to engage with Bader, but as he did so, one of Bader's brothers stretched a surreptitious foot through the ropes of the ring and, unseen by any of the other tribespeople, tripped Raf.

Raf fell and Bader pounced on him, wrapping him in a headlock and pounding him against the ground. What followed was a humiliation, as much to crush Raf's spirit as it was to provide an example to the other members of the tribe. It took weeks for the cuts and bruises to fade and Raf was an object of ridicule every time he passed the ruling family.

He would just bow his head and walk on, fuming.

*

And so Raf spent his days as an outsider within his own tribe—farming with his sister, inventing his weapons and training himself in their use, climbing and hunting alone at the edge of the Badlands. It was during this time that water became scarcer and people started dying in greater numbers.

And then came the day that Raf's sister fell ill with the disease.

Raf hastened to the head family's hut to see what could be done.

A crowd was massing at the entrance. They were gathered around three young men of the head family who were dressed in their finest fighting clothes and bearing weapons.

Raf sighed when he saw who was at the centre of the commotion: Bader. People were handing the tall young warrior sacks of produce and handicrafts.

'What's happening?' Raf stopped a youth hurrying by with a wooden shield in his hands. The boy's name was Timbuk and he was a year younger than Raf. Wide-eyed and eager to please, Timbuk yearned to join the ranks of the head family's warriors. So he acted as their errand boy and they let him, even as they joked about him behind his back.

'Didn't you hear?' Timbuk said breathlessly. 'Last night, Lilibala took ill with the disease.' Lilibala was the chief's only daughter and youngest child, his favourite. 'The chief is sending a war party to demand the Elixir from the trolls! He is sending Bader, both with gifts and swords. The chief is such a man of action.'

'Yes,' Raf said, 'a man of action who has not acted till one of his own was struck down.'

'Bader will save us,' Timbuk said keenly. 'I know he will.'

Timbuk rushed off with the shield, handing it reverently to Bader.

Raf stared at the bustle. The chief of the tribe and his clique of related elders all patted Bader on the back and wished him good fortune.

Raf stared at their fat bodies and then looked at his own skinny form—as the rest of the tribe starved, the chief's family were clearly still eating their fill.

Something in him stirred and he stepped forward and hailed the chief.

'Sir, my sister, she has taken ill,' Raf said loudly.

'As has my beloved daughter,' the chief said. 'Put your faith in Bader. He will show those trolls

that the Northmen are a noble people and demand
of them some of their fabled Elixir.'

'What of the bargain they are said to demand
for use of the Elixir?' Raf asked.

Even he could discern what the bargain was:
you traded yourself for the Elixir; your loved one
survived, but *you* remained with the trolls. It struck
Raf that the head family were not the kind of people
who willingly sacrificed themselves for anyone.

'*We* do not bargain with trolls!' the chief said,
raising his voice so that all could hear. 'Other
tribes may, but the reputation of the Northmen
is a currency that they do not possess! Bader will
bring back the Elixir and our tribe will be cured of
this accursed disease!'

The crowd cheered.

The chief smiled.

Then the war party—Bader and two other
burly young men, with three smaller tribesmen
carrying their gifts and provisions—departed,
heading north out of the valley.

Raf watched them go in silence before returning
to his hovel to tend to his sister.

*

Bader's party never returned.

They were expected back within a week, but soon seven days became ten, then fifteen.

Every day Raf kept watch at the northern edge of the valley, but he saw no sign of Bader or his party.

All the while, Kira's health deteriorated. Her eye sockets grew dark and hollow. The boils on her skin multiplied. Her gums became withered and dry.

Raf tended to her with great devotion, to the point where he had to hold food and water to her mouth just so she could eat and drink.

One evening, Kira smiled weakly at him through her cracked lips. 'I never . . . thought I would see . . . the day when *you* would dote on *me*.' Her little chuckle became a pained, hacking cough.

That night, Raf stroked her hair as she fell asleep. He couldn't stand this. With every passing day she was getting nearer and nearer to death, yet still there was no sign of Bader's war party.

The next afternoon—the sixteenth day after Bader and his warriors had departed—Raf made his decision.

*

That evening, Kira awoke from a restless sleep to find Raf kneeling by the fire filling a rabbit-skin pack.

'Raf. What are you doing?'

'I'm going to Troll Mountain. To get you the Elixir.'

'Raf, no! You can't! You can't give yourself to the trolls in exchange for curing me. How can I live knowing you traded your life for mine?'

Raf turned to her, and she saw a fire in his eyes, a gleam of fierce determination.

'Kira, I didn't say I was going to trade myself for the Elixir. I said I'm going to Troll Mountain to *get* the Elixir. I'm going to steal the Elixir from the trolls.'

Later that evening, long after the last fires in the camp had winked out, by the light of the full moon, Raf slipped away from the small collection of shanties that formed the village of the Northmen.

As he crested one of the higher hills, he looked behind him and saw a glow on the distant southern horizon, far beyond his village: the settlement of the Southmen tribe.

For many generations the Northmen had fought with the Southmen, but few remembered what had actually caused the rivalry. Perhaps it was their base physical differences: the Northmen were fair of skin and hair, while the Southmen had a darker complexion, with long beards, hairy forearms, and bushy eyebrows.

As a child, Raf had been instructed to raise the alarm should he ever see a Southman anywhere near their lands. Sure, Southmen did not steal children in the night, but they were scum, untrustworthy dogs who would steal your crops the moment you turned your back.

It was similar with hobgoblins. Smaller than a man but more cunning and sly, a lone hobgoblin could slip into your hut in the night and steal all of your allocated food from beside your bed. Acting alone, a hobgoblin was a troublesome thief and while its cackling in the night might give a child nightmares, on its own a hobgoblin was of little danger to a human—it would be quick to flight. Larger groups of hobgoblins, however, could be lethal: if a gang of them caught a man and pinned him down, they would eat his flesh while he was still alive. Hobgoblins did not build or make anything. They lived in caves in the mountains or in abandoned places built by others.

Trolls, however, were another matter entirely.

They *did* steal children in the night.

And even a single troll was deadly.

Any news of a rogue troll in the valley triggered great fear and panic. Fires would be lit and a night watch instigated if a rogue troll was known to be about.

If Raf ever saw a troll he'd been told to run away as fast as he could.

*

The trolls lived to the north of the river valley amid some forbidding mountains that, by an accident of geography, sealed off the peninsula on which the valley tribes lived.

The Black Mountains, they were called.

The mountains dominated the landscape, jagged, dark and tall, and always within sight of the valley: a constant reminder to the Northmen, the Southmen and the other minor tribes of the strange foreign culture that held ruthless sway over their lives.

For it was within those mountains that the trolls had blocked the river that flowed into the valley. And by controlling the flow of water to the peoples of the valley, the trolls exacted tribute from them: food and, occasionally, human sacrifices.

Apart from the trolls, the Black Mountains held within them other dangers: isolated clans of hobgoblins and roving packs of mountain wolves.

Between the river valley and those fearful mountains was a ribbon of barren land known as the Badlands.

Once it had been a healthy forest fed by the same river that continued on into the valley, but now the Badlands were little more than a stinking waste of swamps, marshes, and bracken. It was a dead land that conveniently separated the creatures of the mountains and the humans in the valley.

Dawn came as Raf crested the northernmost hill of the river valley and beheld the Black Mountains and the Badlands. A chill wind rushed down from the mountains, bitingly cold.

A tribal elder had once told Raf that the trolls liked the cold, needed it, that they couldn't survive in warmer climes—which was why they stayed in the mountains and sourced tribute from the human tribes.

For a long moment Raf stood on the summit of that last hill, caught between two worlds: the familiar world of his valley and the unknown world before him.

Sure, he had practised with his weapons at the edge of the Badlands, but he had never dared to venture any kind of substantial distance into them.

But today is different, he thought. *Today I must.*

He looked behind him and beheld his own valley again, with the scar of the dead river running down its length, and for a moment he doubted his mission and considered going back—

No. He was going to do this.

He was going to do this for his sister.

And so, with a deep breath, Raf turned toward the Badlands and stepped out of his old world.

An old dirt track crossed the Badlands, twisting and turning through the barren landscape.

Once the track had been well used and clear, but now weeds dominated it. At times the path disappeared completely beneath the undergrowth or pools of rainwater and Raf had to rediscover it further on.

Raf walked along the track, flanked on both sides by forests of thorns. Occasionally, with a suddenness that would make him jump, birds took flight or an unseen ground animal would scurry through the brush.

If he kept up a good pace, he estimated it would take him three days to cross the Badlands.

On the first night, he camped by the putrid muddy stream and lit a small fire. No sooner was it ablaze than Raf saw something in the tree line.

A black wolf, staring at him with unblinking eyes.

Raf didn't know how long it had been there. His hand moved to his axe.

The wolf just stood with its head bent low, watching him. Then it slowly opened its jaws, revealing long deadly fangs, and growled—

The second wolf came exploding out of the thorn bushes to Raf's left.

Raf turned, raising his axe, just in time to be hit by the beast and thrown to the ground. It landed right on top of him. Raf struggled. But the animal didn't move. It had his axe-blade lodged deep in its chest.

Then the first wolf attacked, bounding toward him as he lay defenseless on the ground. It leaped—

Shwap!

—only to drop out of the air and slide to the muddy ground right in front of Raf, with an arrow protruding from its rib cage.

Raf spun to see a dark figure standing at the edge of the clearing, a crossbow pressed against his shoulder.

'Lowland wolves,' the figure said, reloading his weapon. 'They've been following you for several hours now. The birds knew they were here. That's why they took flight. You were lucky these were lowlanders. They're smaller than mountain wolves and not nearly as aggressive.'

'*Not* as aggressive?' Raf said.

'Oh no.' The figure stepped into the light, revealing himself to be a little old man. 'A pack of mountain wolves wouldn't have bothered stalking you. They would have just killed you on sight.'

He said this plainly, in the manner of one expressing the most rudimentary of facts.

Raf stared at the old man. He was, quite simply, the oldest person Raf had ever seen, far older than any of his tribe's elders. This man had a long greying beard, oddly pointed eyes, and he wore a curious hat made of wicker. In his hands he held the now-reloaded crossbow, poised and ready.

'Who are you?' Raf asked.

'I am Ko,' the old man said pleasantly. 'I live here in the Badlands on my own, in the tranquillity that only solitude can provide.'

As a child, Raf had heard the older boys speak of a hermit who lived in the Badlands, a stranger from the east who worked magic and evil spells. Perhaps this was he.

Raf said, 'Hello, Ko. My name is—'

'You are Raf, brother of Kira. Occasionally, you hunt at the periphery of these lands and sometimes you fight shadows using weapons of your own devise. I have watched you often.'

'You have?'

'Oh, yes, and I have enjoyed doing so.' Ko smiled. 'You are a keen inventor. You create a weapon and then figure out how to use it by experimentation. It is nice to see one so young trying to create new things.'

Raf cocked his head. 'When I showed one of my weapons to my chieftain, he laughed and called me foolish.'

Ko sighed. 'I have seen other members of your tribe in these lands. It is they who are the fools. Your ideas are novel and clever.'

'You've seen my people?' Raf said with a start. 'Did you happen to see a six-man party come through here about sixteen days ago? Three warriors and three porters?'

'Of course I did. How could I not? They made no attempt to travel in silence. They spoke much about the trolls before they ventured into the mountains.'

'Did you see them *return*?'

'No. I did not.'

'You say you heard them,' Raf said, 'but you did not speak to them?'

'Often, I shadow folk who pass through these lands. The ability to move silently and unnoticed is a skill my people value highly. When I was a younger man, if I may speak immodestly, I was very good at the art of silent movement.'

Looking at the old man, Raf decided that that must have been a very long time ago.

'How did you know my name?' he asked.

Ko smiled again. 'Your sister calls it when she comes searching for you at the end of the day. And you use hers when you rejoin her. She frets when you go out alone.'

'Oh.'

'And what causes you to be venturing this far into the Badlands, young Raf? This is beyond your usual range. You seem prepared for a sizable journey.'

'My sister is ill with the sickness. I am going to Troll Mountain to procure the Elixir for her.'

'You plan to trade your life for hers?' The old man seemed surprised. 'To grant the trolls their cruel bargain?'

'I plan to procure the Elixir for my sister,' Raf repeated.

'Oh. I see.'

The old man examined Raf closely, as if he was deciding whether or not to say something.

'Raf,' he said at last, 'you are a clever boy, brighter than any of the others I have seen from your tribe. But cleverness is not wisdom. To be clever is to be able to think of new things, methods, ideas. This is most commendable and, indeed, the young can be clever. Wisdom, however, comes from experience, from seeing things happen again and again, which is why the young are rarely wise. Would you allow an old man to impart to you some hard-earned wisdom?'

'I would welcome it.'

'When you go in search of elixirs, be sure you know exactly what an elixir is,' Ko said simply.

Raf frowned. 'An elixir is a cure. A liquid one drinks that heals one from a disease.'

'I have said what I have said.' Ko blinked once and slowly. 'I hope it aids you in your quest. I would be saddened if your sister died. She always struck me as a sweet girl who cared for you deeply—'

A wolf howled somewhere.

Raf turned. The old man did, too.

'That,' Ko said, 'is the howl of a mountain wolf. They are coming down from the mountains to hunt.'

Raf stared fearfully out into the darkness.

'They are natural night-time hunters,' Ko said, 'great dogs that can see in the dark as if it were day. But they only come down to the Badlands rarely, when they sense opportunity.' The old man looked outward, as if appraising the night itself. 'Which they clearly do this evening. Were you planning on making camp here tonight?'

'I . . . I was. Why?'

Ko said, 'A few miles from here is the Broken Bridge. Beyond that bridge, in the parts of the Badlands closest to the mountains, rogue trolls lurk in larger numbers. It is only their inability to cross the Broken Bridge that keeps them from penetrating your valley more often than they do.'

'Rogue trolls . . .'

'Normally, you would be safe making camp on this side of the bridge, but with mountain wolves about . . . well, wolves most certainly *can* cross the Broken Bridge. Perhaps you would like to take shelter in my home tonight. It is not much, but it is fortified against predators such as mountain wolves.'

Raf frowned again, considering this.

At that moment, several other wolves answered the first wolf's call, but from the opposite side of the Badlands. The wolves were communicating, hunting as a pack.

Raf turned to the wizened old man and nodded.

'Thank you, sir. I think that would be a very good idea.'

*

Ko lived in a small shack built on stone pilings out in the middle of a stinking swamp. Flies buzzed, frogs burped, and inordinately large snakes occasionally broke the surface of the muddy pond as they slithered by.

To get to the shack, Ko laid out a long plank, using it as a bridge to span the moat of putrid swamp water.

'Mountain wolves will not swim across so foul a swamp as this,' he said as they crossed the plank-bridge.

Ko lifted it up after them. Raf winced at the rank odour of the place.

'You get used to the smell quite quickly,' Ko added cheerfully. 'One of the greatest features of the human brain: the ability to ignore a smell after a short while.'

That evening, by the light of a small fire, Ko and Raf spoke for a long time about many things.

Raf asked Ko about his life in strange faraway lands, while Ko frowned when Raf told him about the Northmen's tribal hierarchy.

'What an awfully backward structure,' Ko said. 'The most successful cultures I have seen do not allow such men to rule. Eventually, people come to realise that for their society to advance they must allow *everyone* to contribute to the best of their talents. The strong, in particular, must choose to serve the group as a whole, not their own interests. Tribes governed by thugs do not advance. They eventually stagnate and die.'

'Tell me,' Raf said, 'do you know anything about this illness?'

'Occasionally sailors from my homeland who went on long voyages would be afflicted by a similar disease. But no cure for it was ever found,' Ko said.

'Do you know how the trolls discovered their Elixir?' Raf asked. 'How can creatures so brutish find a cure while we cannot?'

'No,' Ko said, frowning. 'This I do not know. The mountain trolls in these parts are not known for their cleverness. Their discovery of the Elixir is a most curious thing for which I have no explanation at this time.'

As he said this, Ko picked up Raf's axe. After a moment, he extracted the flint knife hidden within its handle with a delighted grunt.

'Ah, how clever!' But then he said, 'Not all trolls are brutish, Raf. Indeed, some of the varieties of smaller troll have been known to be remarkably intelligent. Here is another piece of wisdom for you: don't judge a whole race by the actions of some of its members. If I were to judge you based on the actions of your fellow tribe members, I might believe you were a boorish oaf who thinks little.'

Raf nodded at that.

Ko added, 'And while a troll is indeed rather brutish in appearance and has a well-armoured hide, it does have a weak spot.'

'What is that?'

'Like the crocodile, a troll has very soft skin under his chin and under his arms,' Ko said.

While Ko inspected Raf's knife, Raf examined Ko's crossbow. He noted its powerful spring-loaded firing mechanism and the small collection of arrows held in notches on its left side—some had sharp points, others bulbous tips filled with ignitable material. He also noticed a length of closely woven gold-coloured rope looped around two hooks on the weapon's right side.

'That is the finest rope I have ever seen,' he said.

Ko nodded. 'It was made by one of my country's best armourers for my old commander, who gave it to me as a parting gift.'

Raf held it beside his own rope. By comparison, his rope looked frayed, crude and primitive. 'I thought mine was good, but this, well . . .'

'Your rope *is* good,' Ko said firmly. 'Because you crafted it with your own hands. And besides, it's rope. As long as it holds your weight, how pretty does it need to be?'

Raf smiled. As he did so, he noticed in the corner of Ko's shack six small green barrels with what appeared to be candlewicks sticking out of their lids. A strange kind of writing was painted on their sides. It read: 火粉末.

Raf nodded at them. 'What is in those barrels?'

'Ah . . .' Ko smiled. 'It is perhaps my people's greatest invention, the secret formula for which I am privileged to know.'

Ko went over to one of the barrels and lifted its lid. He extracted a handful of thick black powder. 'It is called *firepowder*,' he said. 'My old army would use it to hurl heavy iron balls great distances into the ranks of our enemies, to topple their battle elephants and bring down the walls of their fortresses.'

Raf gazed at the black powder. 'The powder catches alight?'

'More than that. If you light their wicks, these barrels will combust mightily, creating most powerful blasts. This strange powder won my country many wars.'

Raf nodded slowly, impressed. 'Firepowder.'

Ko leaned forward. 'Speaking of winning battles, let me give you a third piece of wisdom, my young friend, given you will be fighting your own battle soon: to bring down a four-legged beast, you only need to injure *two* of its legs. This rule applies to battle elephants and mountain wolves alike.'

Raf thought about that as he went to sleep that evening—for later on, outside the thin walls of the shack, beyond the closer noises of the swamp, he heard the rustle of branches and the grunts of a pack of large wolves, very near, and he was glad he had taken up the old man's offer of hospitality.

The next day, Ko offered to accompany Raf on his quest, at least for part of the way.

'I know the Badlands,' he said, 'and I might be able to help you at some of the more difficult swamp crossings.'

Raf was glad of the assistance and over the course of that day, they made excellent progress through the middle regions of the Badlands.

Ko did indeed know the Badlands well. At those times when the path was hidden beneath wide pools that had crept across it, Ko knew where fords lay, saving Raf the many hours it would have taken to skirt the pools.

Ko walked with an easy lope, carrying his crossbow casually in his folded arms.

At one point in their journey, when they had

stopped to eat some lunch, Raf asked, 'How did you come to be in these lands?'

'Oh, I was part of a vast army from the east, led by a great warrior-king. Over the course of a long campaign, we conquered many lands and acquired many treasures.

'I was a medicine man who tended to our soldiers when they were wounded or fell ill. Our army stopped its great journey of conquest a thousand miles to the east of here and when it turned for home, I asked the great king if I might remain in these parts. He granted me my request, and I ventured over many hills and valleys until I settled here in these Badlands with their splendid solitude.'

'You don't like people?' Raf asked.

'I don't like what people do to each other.'

As the sun set at the end of that second day, black shadows extended across the track. The trees seemed to reach out for Raf, their branches gnarled arms, their twigs flexing claws. Ko didn't seem to notice the grimness of their surroundings at all.

As night fell, they came to the old Broken Bridge.

'Broken' was an overly complimentary term, Raf thought as he looked at it.

In truth, it was no bridge at all anymore.

A broad muddy stream cut across the track here, part of the dry river that meandered down to Raf's valley. Over the centuries, in times when the river's flow had been stronger, it had cut a deep gash in the brown landscape, about thirty feet across and fifteen feet deep, with sheer muddy walls. The streambed itself was a muddy bog: moist, brown, and stinking.

At some point in history, someone had bridged the stream, but the bridge had long ago been washed away or its planks pilfered for other uses, so now all that remained in its place were the stone pillars on which it had stood. They spanned the muddy streambed at regular intervals—intervals across which a man could leap with a bounding stride and good balance.

Raf saw another thing in the mud of the streambed.

Footprints.

Only they were not human footprints.

They were larger and deeper than human footprints, the stub-toed prints of trolls.

Ko said, 'The Broken Bridge is a great protector of your river valley, Raf. Trolls do not have the same kind of toes as humans. Theirs are smaller, less dextrous. The chief consequence of this is that trolls do not possess the same level of balance as humans. For a troll to leap from one of these pillars to the next would be a considerable feat, hence the relative infrequency of rogue trolls reaching your valley.'

Raf nodded at the trollprints in the bog. 'The prints only come halfway across the streambed. Why?'

Ko nodded. 'The mud of the streambed is deadly. It is gripping mud, with the texture and malevolence of quicksand. Once you are stuck in it, it slowly takes you under. The prints only come halfway across because by then the unwary troll is hopelessly stuck and the bog swallows him.'

Raf stared at the muddy bog in horror. A bubble popped on its surface, as if it were alive.

'Trolls are far stronger than humans are,' he said. 'But they are not very clever, are they?'

'Apart from the smaller field trolls, yes, that is correct,' Ko said. 'In his ultimate wisdom, the Great Creator made sure that no one creature got every talent. Yes, trolls got immense size and strength, but as compensation for those talents, they have only rudimentary balance and limited intelligence. Humans received ingenuity but little raw strength. Wolves have cunning, and height-ened senses of smell and hearing, but thankfully no opposable thumbs.' Ko smiled wistfully. 'I like to think the Great Creator just wanted to make life in this world interesting.'

Raf looked from the footprints in the mud to the rather sinister terrain on the other side of the Broken Bridge. The forest of thorns on that side seemed thicker, the shadows more menacing.

This was becoming too real. Real wolves, real trolls, real darkness. Cold fear shot through him and for a moment he considered turning back. Boldly venturing out on this quest had seemed a lot easier from his hovel back in the valley.

But then he thought of Kira, dying from the illness, and his resolve returned.

He turned to Ko. 'Are trolls naturally cruel? Ever since I was a child, I have been told that every troll is a monster bent only on feasting on human flesh and wreaking havoc and destruction.'

Ko looked at Raf for a long moment before replying.

'This is a most perceptive question, Raf. Many humans live their entire lives without questioning the "truths" they've been told.'

'And?'

'Despite a mountain troll's commanding physical size, its brain is small, so it is incapable of complex thought. This does not mean, however, that it is incapable of thought. Simple brains just think simply: *eat, kill, gain advantage*, but most of all: *survive*.

'A troll eats humans to survive. A troll exacts tribute from humans to survive. Yes, some trolls *are* cruel, so *their* array of simple thoughts includes more wicked ones like: *dominate, control, hurt, humiliate*.'

'So trolls are not naturally cruel?'

'I don't think so. A significant proportion of humans are cruel but that doesn't mean *all* people are. It is only when the cruel sit in positions of power that cruelty can become accepted. This is as true for trolls as it is for people, but with trolls it can happen more readily as the simple-minded are more easily led.'

Raf thought about this, and then realised something.

'I have seen good people stand silently by while a cruel chieftain beat a tribe member out of sheer spite. The others all accepted the cruelty for fear of being subjected to it themselves, not because they agreed with it. And they were shamed by doing so.'

'Emotions like shame and guilt,' Ko said, 'are the price of having a larger brain: the human knows he can *choose* to stand up to cruelty. The troll can at least claim limited mental faculties.'

Raf said nothing.

'An interesting theoretical discussion,' Ko said. 'I haven't had one of those in years. One of the downsides to being a hermit, I suppose.'

He looked around them. 'Now. We face a choice. We can cross the Broken Bridge now and make some headway into the farthest regions of the Badlands through the night, or we can camp here.'

Raf gazed across the muddy stream at the forbidding terrain on the opposite bank. Night was almost upon them. The full moon was rising above the mountains.

'What about the mountain wolves?' he asked.

Ko shrugged. 'At some point in your journey, you were always going to have to make camp close to the mountains, Raf. A quest would not be a quest if it were easy. If we stay on this side, we will at least have time to make a defence against the wolves. That is the best we can hope for.'

'I think we'll camp here for the night,' Raf said.

'A wise decision,' Ko said.

The sound of something large crashing through the undergrowth woke Raf.

His eyes snapped open. It was still dark. He peered into the moonlit forest around him.

Beside him, Ko was already awake. The old man's head was perfectly still as he listened intently.

The loud crashing noises were coming from the other side of the stream.

Then Raf heard more noises: branches snapping, heavy footsteps pounding on damp earth, and then—suddenly, cutting through the still night air—deep voices.

'*There he is!*'

'*Get him!*'

The voices had a depth that the human voice box cannot reach.

'Trolls?' Raf whispered.

'Yes,' Ko said softly. 'Stay under your blanket and don't move.'

At Ko's suggestion, they had been sleeping just inside the tree line on their side of the muddy stream, without a fire, and with dense layers of leaves covering their blankets, creating a kind of camouflage. Raf huddled under his leaf-covered blanket and stared across the streambed, thankful that it lay between him and whatever was coming through the underbrush—

A huge grey shape burst out of the thorn bushes on the opposite bank and skidded to a halt at the edge of the foul muddy gorge.

Raf gasped at it in wonder.

By the light of the moon, he could see it clearly.

It was six feet tall, with monstrously broad shoulders, monstrously large fists, a monstrously thick neck, and a monstrously solid head.

Indeed, the only things about it that were *not* monstrously sized were its legs—they were disproportionately short, thick, stubby things that held up its huge upper body.

It was a troll.

This was Raf's first glimpse of one since the day his parents had died. Only this troll, despite its imposing size, *was itself frightened.*

It was running for its life.

The troll stood at the edge of the stream, surprised to find its escape route cut off.

The deep voices came again from the thorny forest behind him: *'Here! Tracks! Heading toward the bridge!'*

'Where are you, Düm! We're coming to get you!'

Raf glimpsed flashes of fire in the forest behind the troll: his pursuers were wielding flaming torches.

The fleeing troll looked this way and that, agitated and desperate, before realising that there was no choice but to attempt to cross the muddy stream by way of the Broken Bridge's leftover pillars.

Raf watched as the big creature measured his first leap onto the nearest stone pillar: this appeared to require all of the troll's concentration.

The troll jumped . . .

. . . and landed on the first pillar, swaying precariously but managing to regain its balance.

It was at that moment that his pursuers—four other trolls—rushed out of the forest bearing torches in their enormous hands. If it was at all possible, these trolls were taller and weightier than the first one: they were almost seven feet tall, with broader shoulders and longer arms. But they still had the same stubby legs.

The four pursuers spotted the first troll wobbling desperately on the pillar, high above the mud of the streambed, arms held out for balance.

They howled with laughter.

'Look at him! Stupid Düm!' one guffawed.

'Don't fall in, Düm!' another cackled. 'That foul gunk beneath you is gripping mud!'

Then a third pursuer threw something at the fleeing troll. It bounced off his back, spraying liquid, before falling into the bog.

Raf saw it land in the gripping mud with a soft *gloop*: it was a goblet of some sort. Within seconds, the mud sucked it under.

'Ooh-ahh, Düm! Don't lose your balance!'

Raf frowned. The four pursuers seemed to be, well, drunk.

And indeed, just then, another of them took a lusty swig of foamy liquid from his own goblet before hurling it at the fleeing troll and striking him on the back of the head with it.

'Na-ha! You got him in the head!'

'Well, we know that won't hurt him!'

The fleeing troll—Düm, Raf guessed—risked another leap to the next pillar and made it, again struggling mightily to retain his balance where Raf would have found it quite easy.

The pursuing trolls started throwing other objects at Düm: branches, stones. They bounced off his thick grey hide.

And then one of the pursuers threw a larger rock.

It hit Düm squarely on the side of the head, causing him to lose his balance, and he tumbled from the pillar, falling for fifteen feet, cartwheeling in mid-air, before he landed feet-first in the gripping mud, embedding his legs all the way up to the hip in the viscous goo.

The look of pure fear that flashed across Düm's face when he saw his predicament struck Raf to the core of his being.

It was a look common to all creatures—man, deer, hound and, evidently, trolls—the look of profound terror that follows the realisation that one is moments away from death and there is absolutely no escape.

The four other trolls exploded with laughter when they saw him drop into the mud. Two more rocks were thrown.

One called, 'Maybe you should have thought about this *before* you spoke to Graia. Stupid Düm. See you in the afterworld, you foolish dragger.'

A final rock thunked against Düm's head and the four trolls lumbered off, crashing through the thorn bushes, heading back toward the mountains, leaving the troll named Düm to die.

*

Raf had watched it all with a kind of grim fascination and he was staring at the swaying thorn bushes on the other side of the stream when he heard the troll in the mud whimper forlornly.

Raf slid out from under his leaf-covered blanket and moved to the brink of the stream.

'Raf—!' Ko hissed.

Raf just held up his hand.

He looked down into the bog and saw the troll hopelessly lodged in it, panting as it struggled in vain against the gripping mud. With every movement the troll managed only to sink itself further into the ooze.

It looked pathetic and terrified. It was going to die here, slowly and alone.

'Hey . . .' Raf called.

The troll jerked round in the mud, looking this way and that before it realised the voice had come from the southern side of the muddy stream.

Its fearful eyes found Raf's and in a single instant Raf saw a complex series of thoughts pass through them: this troll needed a *human*'s help, but given the history of human–troll relations, such a thing was unlikely to happen.

'Please help Düm,' it said as it sank another inch into the mud.

Raf looked long and hard at the creature. He thought of his mother in the grip of a wild troll. He had never contemplated that his own first encounter with a troll might involve *saving* one.

'If I help you,' he said, 'you won't hurt me?'

'Düm no hurt. Düm promise no hurt.'

Ko came alongside Raf and whispered, 'Not all trolls fully understand the concept of a debt of gratitude, Raf. If you save him, he may not believe he owes you anything.'

Raf pursed his lips, still thinking.

Ko said, 'This doesn't have to concern you—'

Raf spun to face Ko. 'Yes. It does. I will not stand by and watch a creature die.'

With those words, he pulled out his axe, tied his rope to its handle and, holding the other end of the rope, threw the axe down to the stricken troll.

It landed in the mud next to Düm and he grabbed hold of it.

'Hold on and we'll pull you up,' Raf said.

The troll obeyed and with slow, careful movements, Raf and the far more reluctant Ko pulled him through the gripping mud to their side of the stream. Once Düm was out of the mud and standing on more solid dirt, they used the rope to help him scale the sheer wall of the stream until at last the troll stepped up onto their bank.

He rose to his full height, looming head and shoulders above Raf and Ko.

There was a long pause as he stared at them.

'Düm would be pleased to know your name, so Düm may thank you.'

Raf smiled. 'My name is Raf.'

'Thank you, Raf. Thank you for saving Düm's life.'

Raf, Ko, and Düm were sitting around the remains of the fire. It was very late. The forest was dark and still. Raf stared at the huge troll with wary fascination. Düm looked big and powerful but quiet, not enraged and wild like the troll that had killed his parents.

'Why were those trolls chasing you?' Raf asked.

'Düm refuse challenge, so they chase Düm,' the troll said. 'Try to kill Düm.'

'You refused a challenge?' Raf asked.

Ko explained. 'Troll society is a highly ritual-ised warrior culture. Arguments are often settled by challenging another troll to combat on the Fighting Platform. One cannot refuse such a challenge and combat is a fight to the death.'

Düm nodded sadly. 'Düm only wanted to help Düm's friend Graia.'

'What happened?' Raf asked.

'Düm's friend Graia is she-troll. Graia *beautiful*. Graia always nice to Düm, even though Graia she-troll of high birth and Düm just a dragger.'

'A dragger?' Raf glanced at Ko.

'Draggers are the labourers of the troll world,' Ko explained. 'All day long they drag heavy stone sleds packed with supplies up the side of Troll Mountain.' He lowered his voice to a whisper: 'Draggers are not as bright as the ruling trolls, as you can see from this one's speech.'

Düm went on. 'Yesterday, Düm see Graia crying and ask what wrong. Graia say she betrothed to Troll Prince Turv. Troll Prince Turv is son of Troll King. Very strong troll. Very powerful troll. But Graia no like Troll Prince Turv. She say Turv mean troll and she no want to be betrothed to Turv.

'Since Graia nice she-troll and friend to Düm, Düm seek audience with Troll Prince Turv. Düm tell Turv it make Graia unhappy to be betrothed to Turv and that maybe Turv find other she-troll to marry.'

Düm sighed sadly.

'Turv get very angry with Düm. Turv challenge Düm to combat on Fighting Platform. But Düm not a warrior, Düm only a simple dragger. Düm know that Turv will certainly kill Düm in fight.'

The big troll bowed his head in shame.

'So Düm flee from Troll Mountain and hide in Badlands. Turv send his warrior friends to beat and kill Düm. Warriors track Düm into forest. Lucky for Düm, they plenty drunk and so make much noise. But then Düm reach muddy river here and fall in. Düm surely die in mud if not for Raf throwing rope. That why Düm here.'

Raf looked at him closely. 'The troll prince sent his friends to kill you because you tried to persuade him not to marry a girl?'

Düm nodded.

Ko said, 'As I was saying to you before, because of the size of their brains, trolls are very black and white in their perception of things. They do not see nuance. Even the smallest slight is taken very seriously by a troll. And when one troll challenges another, the challenge *must* be accepted. By fleeing from a formal challenge, our new friend here broke a very serious social taboo. He probably cannot go back now.'

Düm nodded. 'That right. But Düm very thankful to Raf for saving Düm's life. If Düm can help Raf in any way, please allow Düm.'

Raf looked from the troll to the Black Mountains, dark shadows against the night-time sky.

Düm followed his gaze and then turned to Raf, as if he had just realised something. 'What bring Raf so deep into Badlands forest?'

Raf turned back to face him. 'I'm on my way to Troll Mountain, Düm. I'm going there to steal the Elixir.'

Düm's face went pale. 'Wh . . . what?'

'My sister is dying of the disease and the trolls won't release the cure. I have no choice but to go and take it.'

Düm shook his head. 'Master Raf. Please. Düm wish he could help, but after another human chief sent thieves to Troll Mountain to steal Elixir, Troll King doubled guards on all watchtowers leading there. None can approach Troll Mountain now without being seen, not unless . . .'

Raf's eyes narrowed. 'Unless what?'

'Not unless one go through old hobgoblin kingdom,' Düm said. 'Hobgoblins take over old cave system inside mountain east of Troll Mountain. Called Forbidden Mountain. Hobgoblins crafty, shrewd. And can see in dark. Fill tunnels of Forbidden Mountain with booby traps that trolls cannot pass. But now it claimed that hobgoblin kingdom deserted.'

'If it's deserted then we should be able to pass through it unhindered,' Raf said.

'Traps still there,' Düm said, 'and traps still work. Mountain called Forbidden Mountain because trolls forbidden to go there. No troll who go into hobgoblin kingdom ever return.'

'And in my experience,' Ko said ominously, 'no former kingdom is ever truly deserted. Something always moves in to fill the void.'

Raf bit his lip in thought.

Then he said, 'If it's the only way, it's the only way. Düm, you said you wanted to help me. Well, now you can. If you take me through the realm of the hobgoblins and within sight of Troll Mountain, I will consider your debt paid.'

With a worried look, the big troll nodded.

The next day, guided by Düm, Raf and Ko crossed the final section of the Badlands and entered the foothills of the Black Mountains.

Düm was not at all happy to be heading back into troll territory. But since they were veering east and not sticking to the main road that followed the river, and since Raf *had* saved his life, he did it anyway.

As they walked, Raf asked, 'Is there any way an exiled troll can make amends for his crime and be readmitted to troll society?'

Düm said, 'Only one way to undo exile. That is to bring Troll King an offering of fresh human flesh.'

Raf stopped walking. 'What!'

Düm bowed his head. 'Human meat great delicacy for trolls. Especially soft meat of human woman or child. Man-meat very tough, not as nice.' He threw Ko a bashful look: 'And some trolls like marrow of old human bones. Say it has extra flavour.'

'Why wouldn't it?' Ko said flatly.

Something occurred to Raf. 'When exiled in the wilderness, will a troll become hungry very quickly?'

'Oh, yes, Master Raf. Trolls need much food. Hungry troll very sad to see: it get desperate, ravenous, lose all control.'

Raf was thinking of the stories he'd heard about rogue trolls; he also remembered the troll he'd seen abducting his mother. Rogue trolls behaved erratically and killed indiscriminately, and they nearly always took women or children.

Now he knew why: rogue trolls were exiled trolls. When they killed humans, they were doing so either because they were starving or trying to acquire human meat to gain readmittance to the troll tribe.

They wended their way through the foothills.

The landscape was grey and harsh. Any trees that still lived were leafless and dry, eerie skeletons.

Düm said, 'But trolls been dying off for some time now. Trolls suffer from illness. Lucky that old troll, Vilnar, create Elixir and Elixir cure trolls.'

'Vilnar?' Ko looked up at the name. 'Vilnar was the name of a famous field troll, a very wise little troll who experimented in potions and salves. This is the same Vilnar who found your cure?'

'The same,' Düm said.

'I thought Vilnar lived in the northern lands—'

'He did. But when Troll King defeat tribe of field trolls in north and destroy their lands, he bring Vilnar back to Troll Mountain as prisoner to serve as potion-master for him.'

Ko looked stunned. 'Vilnar toils as a slave for your king! Well! That is not right, not right at all—'

They rounded a curve in the rocky path and stopped suddenly.

Two posts flanked the road. Crudely impaled on top of them, mouths open in silent screams, were a pair of troll skulls.

Beyond the grim posts, the path ended at a large stone doorway set into a rock wall. Glyphs and runes were cut into the frame of the ancient doorway, the writings of a civilisation that no living person could now decipher.

A massive unbroken spider web spanned the yawning portal. No one had passed through it in a very long time.

Raf stared at the two impaled skulls. They were large, with tusks on their lower jaws; they looked like an unholy cross between a human skull and a bear skull.

'We have arrived at the realm of the hobgoblins,' Ko said. 'These stakes are a warning from the hobgoblins to their troll neighbours. Are you still sure you want to do this, Raf? If there are hobgoblins still in there, this will not be pleasant.'

Raf didn't hesitate. 'If this is the only way to reach Troll Mountain undetected, then this is the way I must go. You, however, have come far further than you promised, Ko. You have done more than enough for me. There is no need for you to face this danger.'

The old man looked back down the road, as if seeing his little shack in the distance. Then he turned back to face Raf.

'I have indeed come further than I intended,' Ko said. 'And yet now I find myself wanting to come further still. If the trolls of Troll Mountain hold the wise old field troll, Vilnar, as their slave, then this is a wrong that I cannot let stand. If you will have me, I would like to go with you.'

'I would be happy to have you by my side,' Raf said, rather relieved.

He stepped forward and with his flint knife cut a long slit in the spider web sealing the entrance. Then, guided by the firelight of a torch, he led Düm and Ko into the abandoned kingdom of the hobgoblins.

each connected by long straight tunnels that contained other traps. Grim hobgoblin decorations flanked the walls: more troll skulls, and some bear and wolf skulls.

In the first of those caves, Düm found a large wooden sledgehammer near some other mining tools. For a human, it was a large thing, to be wielded with both hands in a slinging over-the-shoulder motion, but Düm held it lightly in one hand.

Flanking the entrance to the next tunnel were the rotting corpses of not one but two trolls: they were both affixed to the wall with their heads sagging and their arms spread wide, their giant hands *nailed* to the stone wall.

Raf stared up at the dead trolls in disgust.

Düm just averted his gaze.

'Hobgoblins did this?' Raf gasped.

'Yes,' Ko said softly.

They passed between the two hideously displayed trolls, entering the narrow stone tunnel beyond them.

'Why would the hobgoblins leave this place?' Raf asked. 'It gives ample shelter and good defence against the trolls.'

Ko said, 'Hobgoblins are most unpleasant creatures, not just because of their cunning but because they only consume. They do not build anything. They do not domesticate animals or plants. They do not *renew*. Hobgoblins live in places built by others and they simply consume what is available for as long as it is available. Then they move on to another place and slowly destroy it. Hobgoblins cannot see beyond the needs of the present moment. They stayed here for as long as it sustained them and then moved on.'

'Are trolls any different?'

'Oh, trolls are much smarter,' Ko said. 'Why, this is the cause of your current dilemma. The trolls deduced that they needed to secure their food and water supply for the future. They did this by damming the river and essentially enslaving the human tribes downstream. They give you just enough water to survive and you give them food. This enforced tribute feeds the trolls with minimal labour on their part. In this regard, the troll is much smarter than the hobgoblin.'

They edged further down the tunnel.

'What exactly is a hobgoblin?' Raf asked.

Ko shrugged. 'Hobgoblins are smaller than

men, but they speak like men. They have hands and feet just like ours but their skin is coarser, leathery, more bristled. If they wcrc not once men then maybe they were once apes—it is as if they are an animal caught halfway between the two, for they share features of both.'

As Ko said this, Raf realised that the tunnel through which they were walking was becoming oddly warm and humid.

They came to a doorway and stepped out into an enormous cavern.

Raf stopped at the sight that met him.

A broad lake of steaming water filled the floor of the mighty space. Raf had seen thermal springs before, but not an entire subterranean lake.

A low wooden bridge spanned the hot lake, giving access to a most unusual feature that dominated the far wall of the massive cavern: a railless stone path cut into the rock wall itself. It switched back and forth up the three-hundred-foot cliff, steadily ascending. Any slip or stumble would result in a fall into the steaming pool at its base. Bored into the huge rock wall beside the path were many man-sized mini-tunnels.

At two places along the path's length there were

ancient guardhouses with drawbridges folding down from them that spanned gaps in the vertiginous walkway. At the moment, the lower of the two drawbridges was folded down and open, while the upper one was folded up, barring passage across its void.

At the very top of the path, Raf saw an imposing stone doorway like the one through which they had entered the old mine: the exit.

Raf stared up in awe at the incredible feat of engineering.

Beside him, Ko wasn't looking at it at all. He was peering at something on the ground nearby. He dropped to his knees to inspect it. 'Oh, dear, this is not good.'

Düm saw what Ko was examining and sniffed with distaste. 'Droppings . . .'

'These are mountain wolf droppings,' Ko said. 'And they are fresh.' He drew his sword with a sharp *zing*.

'Mountain wolves . . .' Raf said. He was already gripping his flint knife.

Düm hefted his sledgehammer.

Ko said, 'Something did move in after the hobgoblins abandoned this place . . .'

A sudden cackle of laughter echoed out from the upper reaches of the cave.

Raf spun.

Düm turned.

'I *seeeeeee* you!' a thin reedy voice called from the darkness.

'I see you, too!' another voice called from another direction.

'I see you three!' a third voice called.

Raf spun again, eyes scanning the cavern, but he saw nothing, no movement.

'You shouldn't have come here,' a lower voice said from somewhere much closer. 'Because now you must die.'

Raf's heart was pounding as he turned once more to face the tunnel through which they had come and abruptly found himself staring into the eyes of a hobgoblin holding a sword.

The sword came rushing at Raf's face.

C *lang!*
    Another sword appeared in front of Raf's nose and parried the incoming blow.

It was Ko's. The old man now stepped in front of Raf and engaged the hobgoblin.

At the same moment, Raf saw three more hobgoblins leap down from fissures in the cavern's walls, armed with rusty swords. Three quickly became six, which quickly became eleven. The gang of hobgoblins came running toward him.

'Raf! Run!' Ko called as his sword clashed with the first hobgoblin's. 'We must get up that path! Go! I will be right behind you!'

Raf ran.

*

Raf and Düm dashed across the low wooden bridge spanning the steaming lake.

Hot moist air wafted around them, rising from the thermal pool. Raf didn't know how hot the lake was, but he guessed it was not far short of scalding.

As he and Düm reached the base of the path on the other side, Ko managed to sidekick the first hobgoblin away and race after them, pursued by the gang of hobgoblins.

Raf looked back in horror at the pursuing creatures.

They were about five feet tall and they ran on their legs and knuckles, clutching rusty swords in tight fists. In the dim light of his torch, he saw their black leather-like skin, pointy ears, snub noses and hunched backs.

They cackled meanly as they ran.

'Fly, little birds!'

'Run, rabbits, run!'

'Oh, yes, we like a good hunt!' their leader called. 'A kill is a kill, but when I bury my blade in a victim who is white with fear, it is so much the sweeter!'

Raf pushed Düm up the path as Ko joined

them. Raf stepped forward to meet the first hobgoblin and the clash of their blades rang loudly.

Raf had the higher ground, which helped him hold off the creature's blows, but the sheer number of hobgoblins was going to be too much for him to handle. Then, suddenly, a huge brown blur *whoosh*ed past Raf and struck the first hobgoblin, sending the little creature flying backward into the lake with a howl. It landed with a splash and screamed in agony as the water scalded its skin. It went under, shrieking.

Raf turned to see Düm swinging his long sledgehammer again. 'Master Raf! Duck!'

Raf ducked and the big hammer *swoosh*ed over his head again and sent another hobgoblin splashing into the sizzling pool.

It gave Raf the moment he needed and he bolted up the path to join Düm and Ko.

And that was how it went: a running sword-battle as Raf, Ko, and Düm ascended the path, pursued by the furious hobgoblins.

They scaled the railless path, clashing swords, parrying blows, always moving, never stopping. They traversed the first drawbridge—the one that was in the open position—but stopped short when they came to the second.

This drawbridge towered high above the floor of the immense cavern, two hundred dizzying feet above the steaming lake.

Raf called out the plan: Ko and Düm would hold off the hobgoblins while he dashed inside the two-storey guardhouse and lowered the drawbridge.

Raf hurried inside the little structure and clambered up a wooden ladder to its upper level. He emerged inside a small chamber, where he beheld a large cogwheel around which the drawbridge's chains were spooled. The chains stretched out through a small rectangular window in the wall.

A low growl made Raf freeze.

Raf turned to see a large shape emerging slowly from the darkness . . .

It was a mountain wolf.

Wait. No.

It was three.

They stepped out from the shadows of the chamber. They were massive, their shoulders easily four feet off the ground. Their eyes were pitiless, their fangs cruel.

Raf didn't stop to stare. He dived for the cog-wheel and released its lever, causing the cogwheel to spin furiously and the drawbridge outside to fall and land on the other side of the void with a loud *bang!*

Then Raf ran for the window through which the chains exited the chamber—just as a hobgoblin appeared on the ladder poking up through the floor and raised his sword, only to be bowled off his feet by one of the wolves. The wolf proceeded to tear the hobgoblin to shreds as Raf grabbed a chain and slid down it, out of the chamber.

*

Ko and Düm stepped backward across the draw-bridge, fending off the hobgoblins as Raf came sliding down one of the drawbridge's chains, overtaking them.

Düm swiped a hobgoblin off the bridge, send-ing the creature flying two hundred feet down to the pool, a high-pitched shriek following it all the way down.

But then the three mountain wolves emerged behind the hobgoblins and the goblins didn't know what to do—suddenly, they were hemmed in both in front and behind by deadly enemies.

'Düm!' Raf called as they stepped off the bridge and onto the path again. 'Destroy the bridge!'

Düm held the big hammer aloft and brought it down on the brackets where the chains were attached to the drawbridge. Two blows and the brackets came loose. Three more and the bridge fell from its chains, plummeting down the rock wall, taking three hobgoblins and one mountain wolf with it.

The remaining hobgoblins were left on the guardhouse-side of the void, with the two remaining wolves. Their fate would not be kind. The wolves pounced on them and the hobgoblins' death screams filled the air.

Raf sucked in a deep breath.

He and the others were safe on their side of the void. With a final look back at the realm of the hobgoblins, he ascended the last few turns of the path and disappeared through the ornate door at its summit.

*

Moments later, he, Ko and Düm emerged from the mine onto a small ledge cut into the side of Forbidden Mountain.

Raf was about to ask Düm how far it was from here to Troll Mountain, when he stopped himself. He didn't need to. The ledge on which he stood faced to the north-west, and laid out before him was the most spectacular and sinister sight he had ever seen in his life.

He was looking at Troll Mountain.

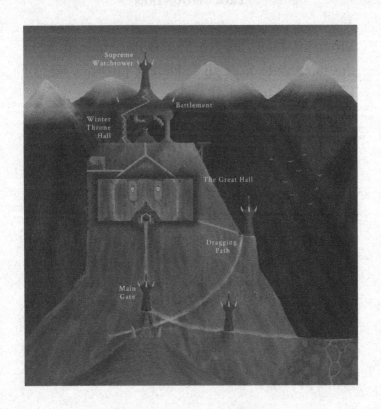

FRONT VIEW (FACING NORTH)
TROLL MOUNTAIN

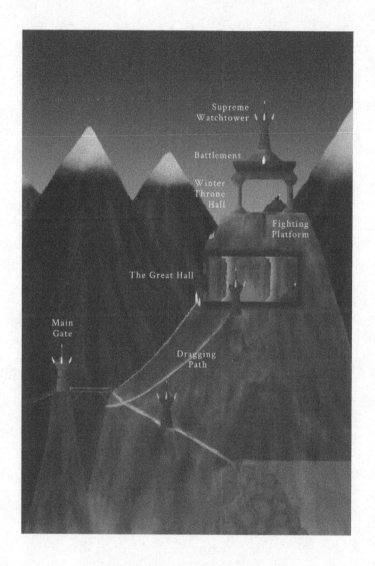

SIDE VIEW (FACING WEST)
TROLL MOUNTAIN

The sight took Raf's breath away.

It was magnificent. It made the realm of the hobgoblins look like an anthill.

From his position to the south-east of it, Troll Mountain stood before him like a giant, rising boldly out of the middle of a circular canyon, surrounded by lesser peaks. And while all the mountains around it were as black as the night, it was of a different colour, a powerful deep grey.

Access to the mountain appeared to be from one point only, a long swooping rope-bridge that stretched from a small stair-equipped pinnacle to the mountain.

The rope-bridge met Troll Mountain at a heavily fortified watchtower that, according to Düm, was known as the Main Gate. As was the trolls' custom, this watchtower—like all the other ones Raf could see on the mountain—was adorned with curved wooden tusks so that it appeared to have frightening horns.

A long and very magnificent staircase rose directly from the Main Gate to an arched doorway situated in the exact heart of the mountain. Flanking this arch were a pair of high ornate windows sunken into the stone.

'Behind arch and windows is Great Hall of the Mountain King,' Düm said solemnly. 'Is where Troll King holds court.'

At the summit of the mountain was a stupendous structure—a wide open-air space dominated by an elevated throne. Four immense pillars sculpted from the actual rock of the mountain supported a roof-like structure that, it seemed to Raf, had once been the original peak of the mountain. Two banners mounted above the open-air throne flapped and fluttered in the gusts of the mountain range.

'That king's Winter Throne Hall,' Düm said. 'During colder months, Troll King holds court up there. Trolls like cold.'

'What's that thing sticking out from the side of it?' Raf asked.

Jutting out from the eastern edge of this open-air space, high above the flank of the mountain, was a circular wooden platform, constructed so that it was level with the space but separated from it by a gap of about ten feet.

'Is Fighting Platform,' Düm said quietly. 'Is where challenges are settled.' The big troll lowered his eyes, reminded of his shame.

Raf looked further up the magnificent mountain.

Above the king's winter throne, encircling the summit of the mountain like a crown, was a crenellated battlement. The tiny figures of two trolls could be seen patrolling it.

Higher still above this battlement, at the mountain's absolute summit, was a final watchtower that looked out over the entire mountain range. It was called the Supreme Watchtower, Düm said. A flag fluttered from its flagpole three thousand feet above the great mount's base.

Down at that base, Raf saw a crude dam constructed of hundreds of troll-stacked boulders. A huge body of water had backed up behind the dam but only a thin waterfall poured over it—this was the dam that blocked up the river.

The dam's meagre waterfall fed a muddy moat that all but encircled the mountain. It appeared to be a bog of gripping mud like the one Raf had seen at the Broken Bridge—only this bog ringed the mountain on three sides. The lake behind the dam protected the fourth side.

Raf gazed in awe at the stupendous mountain.

'How could trolls build such a wonder?' he asked.

Düm said, 'Trolls no build Troll Mountain. Trolls find it deserted many years ago. So trolls just move in and make it theirs.'

Raf threw a questioning glance at Ko.

The old man shrugged. 'The work of the same race of men who dug the mine that became the hobgoblins' kingdom. They built great watchtowers like this from which they could look out over their vast empire. But then they suddenly retreated south, leaving their watchtowers empty.'

Atop every watchtower on the mountain—in addition to the horns the trolls had added—were small glowing fires.

'What are they?' Raf asked.

'All's Well fires,' Düm said. 'If a watchtower's fire burns, then all is well at watchtower. If fire goes out, then trolls know something wrong at that tower.'

Ko added, 'Another creation of the original builders. Those who rule by force soon find that they have many enemies.'

Raf turned back to face the mountain.

'Düm,' he said. 'I thank you for bringing me here and explaining these things to me. I have just one more question for you and when you answer it you may consider yourself relieved of your debt.'

'Yes, Master Raf.'

'Where does your king keep his fabled Elixir?'

Düm swallowed. 'Düm should not tell, but Düm owe Master Raf life debt . . .' He paused, wrestling with this dilemma, but then said, 'Life debt *is* life debt. Elixir is kept in most secure place in Troll Mountain: in Supreme Watchtower, at summit of mountain, higher even than winter throne. That is where king keep wise old troll Vilnar imprisoned, to work on his potions. King have Vilnar guarded day and night. You see guards up there now.' He nodded at the two tiny figures patrolling the battlement ringing the summit of the mountain.

Raf gazed intently at the highest watchtower.

'Master Raf,' Düm said. 'Not even trolls can get into Supreme Watchtower. If you are discovered in Supreme Watchtower stealing Elixir, trolls rip you limb from limb and eat you while you watch.'

Raf said, 'My sister is dying, Düm. So are my people.' His jaw tightened. 'I have no choice.'

Raf then kneeled and extracted some yams from his pack and bit into them hungrily. He figured he should eat now because he'd need energy later.

'Young Raf,' Ko said, 'forgive me, it's been a long while since I had the flush of youthful confidence, but how exactly do you intend to get across to the mountain undetected?'

Raf jerked his chin at the rope-bridge, spoke with his mouth full. 'I'm going to use the trolls' very own bridge.'

That night, an hour after midnight, Raf made his move. The evening was bright and clear and the full moon illuminated the landscape.

Düm had told Raf that trolls usually slept between midnight and dawn, often in a state of substantial inebriation. That was Raf's window of opportunity.

Leaving Düm and Ko on the hobgoblin mountain to the east, Raf skulked down to the pinnacle which held up one end of the rope-bridge that gave access to Troll Mountain.

The All's Well fire burned brightly atop the watchtower on the pinnacle and Raf saw the shadows of two guard-trolls patrolling the tower's uppermost level. Beyond the pinnacle, Troll Mountain loomed in the moonlight.

Using his rope, a hook and his considerable climbing skills, Raf scaled the side of the pinnacle out of the view of the trolls on its watchtower.

At length, he came to the rope-bridge, approaching it from below. He did indeed intend to use it to get to the mountain, but he wasn't going to cross it in the usual way. The bridge hung from a pair of sturdy anchor-posts. Raf noticed that each anchor-post was decorated with an impaled human skull. Trolls and hobgoblins, it appeared, used similar methods to instill fear in their visitors.

Arriving at the rocky shoulder under those anchor-posts, Raf wound up his home-made rope and slung it over his shoulders.

As he did so, he looked up at the underside of the rope-bridge and, for a brief moment, paused.

This is it, he thought. *My last chance to change my mind. My last chance to turn back.*

'You can do this,' he whispered aloud to himself.

And so, taking one final deep breath, he jumped up and gripped the first slat of the long swooping rope-bridge; then he swung across to the next slat, gripping it one-handed with his fingertips.

Thus Raf set out across the rope-bridge, hanging from its underside, swinging from slat to slat, but always moving in a careful, slow way so as not to make the bridge wobble and attract the attention of the guard-trolls on the first watchtower.

His feet dangled above the rocky gorge and the boggy mud moat hundreds of feet below, and for a brief instant he glanced down and saw the immense drop and his heart began to race.

He whipped up his eyes and again breathed, 'You can do this, Raf. You can do this.'

After that, he didn't look down again. With every swing of his arms, he only had eyes for the other end of the bridge.

*

Only two watchers observed Raf crossing the bridge in this daring way: Ko and Düm, from a quarter of a mile away.

Ko held his breath as he watched the tiny figure swing from slat to slat, high above the deadly fall.

Düm was amazed. 'Master Raf clever. Düm would never have thought of crossing bridge like that. Mind you, Düm much heavier.'

Ko kept watching Raf as he replied, 'Yes, he is very clever. I just hope that he will also use some wisdom as his mission progresses into a far more dangerous stage.'

*

At length Raf came to the mountain end of the rope-bridge. There he dismounted onto a shoulder of rock underneath the second troll watchtower, the one Düm had called the Main Gate.

The Main Gate was erected on a small stone outcropping—a mini-pinnacle of sorts—that jutted out from the main body of the mountain, and it too bore a glowing All's Well fire on its roof.

Raf climbed *down* this mini-pinnacle and then crossed a shallow ravine connecting it to the mountain.

This took extra time—it would have been faster to swing underneath the two strong-looking wooden bridges connecting the Main Gate directly to Troll Mountain—but Raf preferred to take a detour rather than risk being detected by any stray troll eye.

With a final jump, Raf landed for the first time on the surface of Troll Mountain.

He looked up.

The great rocky behemoth rose above him, soaring into the star-filled sky, the Supreme Watchtower at its summit silhouetted against the glorious full moon.

Raf swallowed as he eyed the glowing All's Well fire on it.

Then he bent his head and commenced the long climb upward.

Carefully and silently, Raf scaled Troll Mountain. He moved with tremendous caution, making sure not to dislodge any loose stones or rocks—in the eerie silence of the night, a bouncing stone would ring out like a bell.

He scaled the mountain in a zigzagging fashion. At first, this motion took him westward, but for some unknown reason, the western flank of the mountain became sheer and vertical very quickly, so he traversed to the eastern side. It turned out to be far more climbable and had the added bonus of offering more concealment within its crags.

A short way up the eastern flank, Raf came to a paved stone path, worn smooth from constant use. It stretched from the Main Gate up to a side doorway halfway up the mountain.

According to Düm, this path (and another that led from the Main Gate down to the trolls' dam) was used for dragging stone sleds filled with food from the lowlands and water from the dam to the Mountain King's halls.

This was Düm's job as a dragger—the lowest of the low in troll society. All day, every day, he and the other draggers pulled the heavy sleds up the paved path to a kitchen area adjoining the Great Hall.

Düm had also said that low-born trolls, when returning to the mountain, were only allowed to walk up these paths. High-born trolls—the king's family and the families he favoured—could use the more direct route to the Great Hall: the magnificent staircase that rose in a dead-straight line from the Main Gate to the hall's arched doorway on the front face of the mountain.

Raf didn't dare step out onto the path. Rather, he kept within the crags on its upper side and ascended the mountain parallel to it.

*

Further up the Dragging Path, Raf beheld one last watchtower, this one perched two-thirds of the way up the mountain, on its rear corner, facing north-east.

To avoid being spotted by its guards, he bent back around toward the front face of the mountain, climbing close to the corner spine of the great peak, roughly equidistant from the Main Gate and this watchtower, moving carefully, using the folds of the rocky slope to conceal his progress.

At one point in his journey up the front face, he came within twenty yards of one of the high stone windows that opened out from the Great Hall.

Raf wanted to peek inside it, but he didn't dare. He could hear deep snoring sounds within, even from this distance. It was the sound of many trolls sleeping. With their great noses, it seemed trolls were loud snorers.

He climbed ever higher.

A short way up from the window, he came across a small shelf cut into the mountainside, within which was a curious object.

It was a pedestal of some kind.

A monument.

It was cut from beautiful black stone and inscribed on it were words in an ancient language that Raf did not know. Had he been able to comprehend them, he would have read:

THIS STONE COMMEMORATES THE COMPLETION OF THE GREAT WATCHTOWER OF THE NORTH, SEAT OF POWER FOR THE GOVERNOR OF THESE LANDS.

LOOK UPON IT, ENEMIES OF OUR GLORIOUS EMPIRE, AND TREMBLE.

WE SHALL RULE THESE LANDS AND THE PEOPLE IN THEM FOR A THOUSAND YEARS.

The pedestal had the same look to it as the rock-cut doorways in the hobgoblin kingdom—it had been made by that same civilisation of clever men.

A deep crack, however, presumably the result of a blow from a troll hammer, split the monument down the middle. Troll graffiti covered it.

Raf moved on.

Further up, about a hundred feet below the flat floor of the king's open-air Winter Throne Hall, Raf peeped over a rocky crag to discover a most sickening sight.

He saw a set of sharp wooden stakes, a forest of the things, on which were impaled the bloody corpses of trolls and people. All of the dead bodies were in advanced states of decay—the vultures of the mountains had fed on them.

Raf looked upward and saw, directly above the grisly collection of stakes, the southern edge of the Winter Throne Hall.

These poor souls—humans and trolls alike—had been *thrown* down here . . .

Raf looked at one of the fresher corpses more closely and recognised something about it.

This corpse wore the distinctive wooden necklace of an elder of his tribe. He had been a Northman!

Then, to his horror, Raf realised that this man had been one of the two elders who had originally been sent to parley with the trolls when they had cut off the river flow—the two elders who had never returned.

Raf stared at the corpses for a long time before he continued on up the slope.

*

As Raf scaled the mountain, Ko and Düm continued to watch his progress from their ledge.

It was hard to follow him in the gloom, especially when he disappeared behind a crag, but since they knew his objective—the summit—they were able to keep track of him.

'Are there any *other* troll tribes that you know of?' Ko asked Düm as they watched Raf step around the stakes beneath the Winter Throne Hall.

'No,' Düm said sadly. 'We last troll tribe.'

'Really? The last one?'

'Yes. We mainly mountain trolls with a few field trolls and cave trolls. They joined our tribe when their tribes failed. Every year our tribe get smaller.'

'Why is that, do you think?' Ko was genuinely curious.

Düm shrugged. 'Trolls very simple. Enjoy fighting and sporting and not doing much work. Toughest trolls rule and take wives and eat most food. Strongest troll is king.

'So lowly troll happy when wife give birth to big strong boy. Troll sad when wife give birth to she-troll or runt. Often baby she-trolls and runts killed by parents, because they no use in troll tribe. Only boys useful.'

Ko frowned. 'Does that mean you have few females and many males?'

'Yes. That right.'

'Do the males compete for the females?'

'As Düm already say, trolls enjoy fighting. Dispute over she-troll just another reason to have fight. Yes, many fights over that.'

'I see,' Ko said darkly. 'What about the smart trolls? I was under the impression that smaller trolls were quite clever and inventive.'

'This true. Wise trolls often smaller trolls, runt trolls. But now few of them. Some time ago troll kings begin to dislike wise trolls, because they often disagree with king, say king doing wrong thing. But king no want to look like fool so he sometimes throw troublesome wise troll off top of mountain. Many recent kings do this. Now king no longer disagreed with.'

'But without clever tribe members,' Ko said, 'how does your society develop new ways of doing things?'

Düm shrugged again. 'Trolls just keep doing things the way they always been done. Fight as have always fought. No need to farm, since trolls take tribute from humans. Düm not even know how to farm. Düm just know how to drag, drag food and water up Dragging Path. Senior trolls spend most days lazing and drinking and having death fights for sport.'

Ko didn't speak for a long time.

Then he turned to face Düm.

'Is this what happened to the other troll tribes?' he asked.

'Düm not know. Düm just humble worker troll. But some draggers come to Troll Mountain from other failed tribes and, yes, them say same things happen in their tribes.'

Ko gazed out at Troll Mountain.

'Your race is dying and it doesn't even know it,' he said softly. 'Your very culture is killing you off. Within a generation or two, there will be no more trolls walking the earth.'

There was a short silence.

Then Düm nodded at Raf on the mountain.

'What about Master Raf? If trolls catch him, they be very angry. *Very* angry.'

Ko nodded. 'All we can do now is keep an eye on him. But if our young friend is not back by morning, we must assume he has been captured.'

'And if he captured? Then what? Master Raf nice human. Save Düm's life when no have to. Seem bad if he be left to die among trolls.'

'I'm inclined to agree with you,' Ko said. 'There is something about that boy that I like a lot. He's different from the other members of his tribe. He has a future while they do not. I would not like to see him meet a gruesome end.'

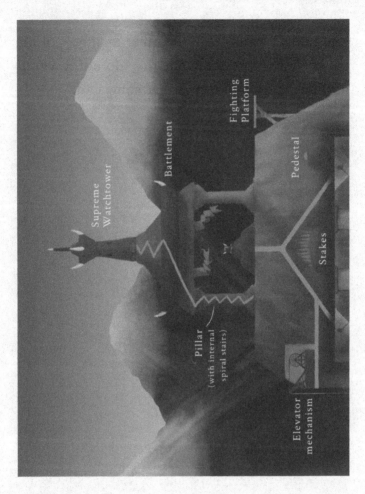

THE WINTER THRONE HALL

After three hours of strenuous climbing, Raf arrived at the upper reaches of Troll Mountain.

Crawling over the lip, he slid up onto the flat stone floor of the open-air Winter Throne Hall and stood.

Raf's jaw dropped.

It was an incredible space: wide and magnificent, even in the eerie darkness of the night. The smooth stone floor, polished to a dazzling sheen, reflected the silver glow of the moon. Four thick, colossal pillars held up the hall's ceiling and, above that, the summit of the mountain.

In the middle of the space, rising on a many-stepped podium, was the king's winter throne. Two long banners made of thick cloth hung from the roof behind the throne, framing it.

Raf noticed a single stairway that burrowed into the polished floor, leading down into the mountain. But there was no obvious staircase going *up*, giving access to the mountain's summit. Perhaps there was a hidden stairway somewhere.

It didn't matter. He wasn't planning to use it anyway.

Raf dashed across the wide polished floor and quickly ascended the massive podium until he stood before the king's winter throne.

(An inscription on it read, in the same ancient language Raf had seen on the monument: THE SEAT OF POWER OF THE NORTHERN GOVERNOR: ALL THAT CAN BE SEEN FROM HERE, HE GOVERNS IN THE NAME OF THE GLORIOUS EMPEROR [UNREADABLE], ALL HAIL HIM, RULER OF THE WORLD.)

Raf was about to grab hold of one of the banners that hung behind the throne and climb up it, when he saw the view from the throne.

It took his breath away.

Beyond the jagged peaks of the nearby lesser mountains, he saw the landscape to the south: the Badlands, his own river valley, and beyond that, the vast southern sea, glimmering in the blue moonlight.

As he gazed out at the magnificent vista, he cursed the cruel trick of geography that allowed the trolls to keep a stranglehold over the valley tribes.

Raf had once asked one of the elders why the Northmen didn't flee to the north of the mountains and escape the tyranny of the trolls.

The elder had smacked him over the head, hard. 'Silly boy! Do you not pay attention when the traditional stories are told? As everyone knows, there are no habitable lands beyond the mountains. There are just more mountains, stretching away to the earth's end.'

Recalling those words, Raf turned around and faced north, expecting to see an endless range of mount—

Wait a moment.

Raf frowned as he gazed northward.

From this vantage point, he could see *beyond* the jagged peaks of the mountain range, and what he saw shocked him.

The Black Mountains did not go on forever.

In fact, they ended quite abruptly only a short distance from Troll Mountain. And beyond the mountain peaks, Raf saw broad sweeping plains, rolling hills and grassy vales, stretching away to the north as far as the eye could see.

'There *is* more land out there . . .' Raf gasped. 'The traditional stories were wrong . . .'

He wondered how the stories could have got it so wrong. Who had created them? And had anyone ever actually checked their accuracy? Or were they accepted simply because they were old and passed on by generations of elders?

Raf shook away these thoughts and returned to the mission at hand—he had to be off the mountain by dawn, before the sun removed the cover of darkness.

He grabbed one of the long banners hanging from the ceiling behind the throne and, moving nimbly hand over hand, scaled the banner and arrived at the rocky uppermost section of the mountain.

Peering upward, Raf spied the thick battlement ringing the summit.

Two guards patrolled it.

He could tell from their postures that they were idle, bored: they clearly didn't believe any intruder could—or would even dare—get this high up the mountain.

Raf saw them stroll away, chatting, with their backs to him—and so he seized the opportunity and darted from cover, scampering up and over the battlement before quickly scaling the last twenty yards of rocky ground that led to the tower at the absolute summit of Troll Mountain: the Supreme Watchtower.

*

Of course, the Supreme Watchtower had no external doors on its brick-walled flanks. Access to it was only available from within.

But given it had once been a working watch-tower, Raf guessed correctly that it would have a door up on the lookout platform at its peak.

No sentries patrolled that platform, since the watchtower was now only used to keep the wise old troll Vilnar imprisoned.

Raf flung his trusty rope up over the crenellations of the Supreme Watchtower's parapet and, hanging from it, scaled the lofty tower with the peaks of all the neighbouring mountains far below him.

At length, Raf slid over the crenellated plat-form and beheld a thick wooden door leading into the Supreme Watchtower.

With a final deep breath, Raf opened the door and stepped inside.

Raf found himself in a small guardroom lit with candles: a room that had been converted into a laboratory.

Thick wooden benchtops were covered with jars, pots, and barrels, all of which were filled with bubbling, steaming liquids. On long shelves sat unruly clusters of flowers, fruits, and vegetables; garlic and onions hung from strings.

In the floor in the centre of the guardroom was a wooden ladder that led to lower levels.

And in the midst of it all, snoring loudly, fast asleep in a chair, was a small wrinkled old troll.

*

Raf stared at the old troll in wonder.

He had never seen a troll like him. He was

smaller than the others, shorter even than Raf was. And he had reedy arms and thin knock-knees. His nose was long and beaky, with several warts, and he had a long white beard on his chin and wild bushy eyebrows. A field troll.

As Raf peered in wonderment, the troll snorted suddenly, making him jump.

But it was well and truly asleep.

Raf realised with a thrill that this was his chance: to steal the Elixir and get away from Troll Mountain unnoticed.

If he could find the Elixir now and leave this tower without waking the old troll, he could be out of the mountains by morning and home with the cure within days.

Moving slowly and carefully so as not to make the slightest sound, Raf went over to the laboratory's benches, scanning them for the Elixir.

There.

Three small glass bottles stood on a table off to one side, all on their own, separated from the clutter of the rest of the room.

They were all filled with the same amber liquid and each bottle was of far higher quality than any of the other vessels in the laboratory. Apart from the dry husks of several discarded lemons and limes beside them, the benchtop around the three bottles was empty. Clearly, these three bottles were special.

Raf stood before them, gazing at the all-powerful Elixir.

Damn the trolls, he thought. He'd take all three.

He stepped forward, his foot landing on an ancient floorboard.

It creaked . . .

. . . and the old troll awoke mid-snore, snapping up, looking around in a muddle. 'What—? Who—oh my—how did you get in here!'

Raf stood erect, somehow finding nobility in being discovered. 'I come from the valley you trolls keep under your thumb—'

The little old troll ignored him, rushing past him to the door through which Raf had entered the tower.

He crouched by the doorframe, looking down at the floor beside it. 'You silly fool—!'

'I seek the magic Elixir,' Raf said desperately. 'My people are dying. Please do not raise the alarm . . .'

The old troll turned, pointing to a mechanism in the floor by the door: a weighted rope plunged down into a hole in the floorstones there.

'My young friend, I'm sorry to inform you that the alarm has already been raised.' He spoke far more eloquently than Düm or the guards did. 'The Troll King keeps me prisoner here. I cannot even go outside for air without his knowing it. When you opened that door, a stone attached to this rope was released. It has already fallen down its hole and hit a bell in the guardroom below. The king's guards *already know something is amiss*. They will be here any moment!'

'No . . . no . . .' Raf's mind was racing. 'I can take you with me then,' he said quickly. 'You are Vilnar, are you not? My name is Raf and I am a friend of Ko's, the old hermit of the Badlands. He speaks highly of you.'

The troll looked at him askance.

'I do indeed know Ko. He is a fine and wise man. And you, young man, you scaled this guarded mountain to steal the Elixir for your people? And now you offer to release me from my confinement, even though I am a troll. What kind of hero are you?'

'I'm no hero, I'm just—'

'Nevertheless, you deserve something for your efforts, even if you are ultimately to end up in the king's belly. If I cannot give you the Elixir, let me at least give you some knowledge: the Elixir is *not* magical. It is the result of much hard work, *my* hard work conducting experiments in this room.'

Raf heard a door slam somewhere deep within the watchtower, followed by urgent shouts.

His eyes shot to the door through which he had entered: he could get out that way, but he knew that he'd never get past the battlement that ringed the summit. The guards on it would be alerted by now.

Vilnar grabbed Raf's shirt and yanked his face to his own, right up to his wart-covered nose.

'Young man, pay attention! The illness, it is not a curse or an omen or black magic. It comes from a lack of nutrients—nutrients peculiar to lemons, oranges and limes. That is all. Which means the Elixir is not magical either, it is merely a juice made from those same fruits. But if I tell that to my captors, they will kill me and retain my hard-earned knowledge!'

Raf's mind was reeling. His brain was in a panic, thinking only of escape and fleeing, and yet here was this silly old troll giving him a lesson in medicine.

He turned desperately. 'I have to get out of here—'

'That's not going to happen,' a hard voice said from behind him.

Raf spun—

—to see four large guard-trolls step up from the ladder in the floor, great hammers gripped in their fists.

Raf's blood went cold.

His mission was over.

Flanked by the four guards, terrified and alone, Raf was marched down through the Supreme Watchtower, then down a tight spiral staircase concealed within the north-western pillar of the Winter Throne Hall. He emerged from a secret door cut into the base of that pillar, stepping out onto the open-air space. It was still dark. Dawn was a couple of hours away.

'Take this scum to the cells,' the head guard growled to the others. He held Raf's rope and lightweight axe in his huge hands. 'The king sleeps. I shall inform him of this thief when he wakes in the morning.'

Raf was pushed across the Winter Throne Hall and down through some more tunnels cut into the main body of the mountain, before he abruptly emerged into fresh air again, arriving at a wooden platform erected high above the western flank of Troll Mountain.

A large wooden box-like contraption—had he known the word, Raf would have called it an 'elevator'—hung before him, dangling from a thick rope in such a way that it could be lowered through a rectangular hole in the floor of the wooden platform. (Raf couldn't see it, but a huge cogwheel housed in a shack above the platform raised and lowered the elevator when the cogwheel was turned by a single muscular troll.)

Escorted by two guards, Raf was shoved onto the box and lowered down the western face of the mountain.

He recalled that during his ascent he had been unable to scale the western face because it was sheer and vertical.

Now he saw that it was more than that.

The entire western side of the mountain had been smoothed by the hand of some outside agent—man or troll, it didn't matter—so that it formed a perfectly vertical surface.

And now, as he was lowered down that sheer polished rock face, Raf saw that cut into it were shallow recesses. Each recess was shaped like an upside-down triangle, with a sharp point at the base, and inside many of the oddly shaped recesses were . . .

. . . human prisoners.

The cells had no bars. They didn't need them. The drop below their brinks was two thousand feet and at the wall's base was a tangled forest of upwardly pointed stakes.

From what Raf could see, the cells were arranged in a grid formation. There were about thirty cells, widely spaced, in three vertical columns. Roughly half of them were occupied.

Forlorn bearded faces stared out at Raf from the cells as he was lowered past them. The prisoners were mostly men and they appeared emaciated and starved. By virtue of the inverted triangular shape of each cell, the prisoners sat in them awkwardly, curled and hunched.

And then suddenly, among the despairing faces, Raf saw one that he recognised.

'Bader . . . !' he gasped.

The prisoner's eyes sprang open in recognition, but before he could reply, Raf's elevator had gone past him, descending lower still.

Raf was finally deposited in a triangular cell of his own. The elevator withdrew upward, taking the guards with it, but not before one of them gave Raf some parting advice:

'Sleep well, thief. If you cannot sleep, you might consider throwing yourself from your cell before the morning, for when the king sees you tomorrow, you will wish you were dead.'

*

When his captors were gone, Raf sat glumly in his cell, pressed against its sloping walls.

The mountain wind was the only sound.

The triangular walls of the cell were perfectly cut, made of hard polished stone without a chip or a notch. The cell was perhaps seven feet high but only four feet deep. The brink yawned before Raf, rimless and railless. Out of the rear wall of the cell poked many tiny bronze spear-tips which prevented a prisoner from leaning against that wall.

Just sitting hunched over in the upside-down triangular hole was uncomfortable enough, but the combination of the spear-tips and the deadly drop meant that Raf had to sit essentially motionless.

He looked up, whispering in the darkness.

'Bader! Bader! Can you hear me?'

A moment of silence. Then:

'I hear you.' The voice, once haughty and proud, was listless and flat.

'What happened to you and your party?'

'We made our case to the Troll King and the dirty beast imprisoned us for our trouble.'

'What of the other members of your party?'

A pause. The mountain wind whistled.

Bader said, 'So far as I can tell, only I remain. Every now and then, the trolls take a prisoner away for eating or sport. We can hear their gleeful shouts when they gather on the Winter Throne Hall. They leave us here to wither and lose all energy. Then, when we are weary from hunger and thirst, they take us. Once taken away, no prisoner ever returns.'

Raf swallowed.

He spent what remained of that night curled up in his uncomfortable stone hole, staring out at the westward view: beyond the snow-capped peaks of the Black Mountains, he saw the vast northern plains. In other circumstances it would have been beautiful.

At length, dawn broke.

Around mid-morning, they came for him.

THE GREAT HALL OF THE MOUNTAIN KING

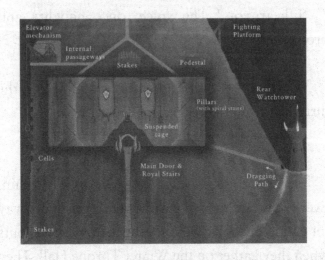

FRONT VIEW

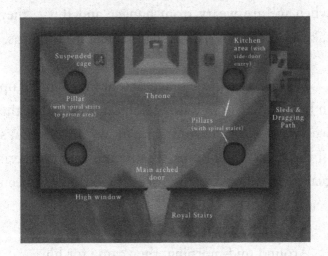

OVERHEAD VIEW

After he stepped off the elevator, Raf was pushed by a pair of guards through a dark horizontal tunnel that delved into Troll Mountain.

He heard shouts and cheers from somewhere.

At the end of the tunnel he came to a fork— he could go up, presumably to the Winter Throne Hall, or down.

He was shoved downward.

The cheering became louder. As he proceeded down a steep passageway, Raf heard a series of dull *thunk*s followed by a chanting of 'Grondo! Grondo!'

A rush of fear shot through Raf's body. Where were they taking him? What had he got himself into?

Then Raf turned a corner and suddenly he found himself standing inside the upper reaches of the vast space that was the Great Hall of the Mountain King.

His breath caught in his throat.

Raf stood at the top of a staircase that wound in an elegant spiral down the outside of a gargantuan stone column. (While the immense column appeared to be an addition to the hall, it—and the three other mighty columns holding up the ceiling—had actually been cut from the mountain itself. Similar spiral staircases wound around the flanks of the other columns.)

In the centre of the immense space was a high pyramidal podium on which stood the Troll King's throne, far larger than the one up on the Winter Throne Hall. A horde of perhaps two hundred trolls was gathered at the foot of the throne, thronging around a pair of trolls who were engaged in combat, cheering and shouting at every blow.

And sitting on the throne, flanked by what appeared to be his sons, his cronies, and a pair of hobgoblin jesters, biting down on a meat-covered bone, contentedly lording over the scene, was the Troll King himself.

*

As Raf was led down the spiral staircase, the two fighting trolls continued their battle, hitting each other's shields with their hammers. Then the bigger troll disarmed the smaller one and broke his wooden shield with a lusty blow and the crowd chanted ever louder, 'Grondo! Grondo!' The big troll started unleashing more blows on the now-defenceless smaller one, knocking him to the ground and pinning him, before turning to the king.

A hush fell over the hall.

All eyes turned to the Troll King.

One of the hobgoblin jesters made a throat-slitting gesture.

The king said simply, 'Kill him, Grondo.'

Grondo's hammer came down on the head of the fallen troll and made a sickening noise.

The crowd roared, the jesters danced, the king smiled, and as the trolls gathered around the victor, Grondo, a pair of worker-trolls dragged the dead body of the vanquished one away.

Grondo was escorted up to the king's throne. He dropped to one knee before the king and bowed his head.

The king stood. 'You are a worthy champion,

Grondo. I thank you for this fine gift of death you have given me on my son's wedding day.'

'It is my honour and privilege, lord,' the champion said.

'Please stay here by my throne today,' the king said, and the crowd gasped for this was clearly an honour. Grondo took his place among the row of courtiers and troll princes standing behind the king, his head held high.

Gripped by his guards, Raf was brought across the floor of the chamber and made to stand directly in front of the king's mighty throne. The huge crowd of trolls stood closely around him, grunting, whispering, and glaring.

Standing in their midst, Raf looked small, frail, and alone and he felt like that, too. He barely reached their shoulders.

'My lord!' called the senior guard. 'I bring you the thief caught on the mountain during the night!'

The king leaned forward, eyeing Raf closely. The crowd of trolls encircling Raf fell silent.

Raf was assessing the Troll King, too. Like all the bigger trolls, the king had a long snout and a pair of tusks jutting up from his protruding lower jaw. Draggers like Düm had flatter faces and no tusks, while field trolls were just small.

As he looked at the king more closely, Raf noticed that he further distinguished himself from the other trolls by wearing foul decorations on his body: a necklace made of human fingerbones, a cloak made of a mountain-wolf pelt, and worst of all, a weapons belt featuring two daggers and a longer blade made of a sharpened human leg bone.

The Troll King spoke.

'I was told about this thief. He was discovered in the Supreme Watchtower, trying to steal the Elixir. No thief has ever made it so far. He must be . . . slippery.'

No one spoke.

The king grinned meanly. 'But not slippery enough.'

The assembled trolls sniggered.

One of the hobgoblin jesters was glaring right at Raf, cruel and hard.

'You are not the first human to attempt to penetrate our stronghold and steal our Elixir, young thief,' the king said. 'Here is another.'

The king held up the meat-covered bone on which he had been gnawing. Raf's blood froze.

'Nothing tastes sweeter than the marrow of an enemy,' the king said. 'And since today is a special day, I think I shall—'

'My tribe is dying,' Raf blurted, and the entire crowd gasped at the sheer gall of someone interrupting the king.

The king looked as if he had been slapped in the face.

'You cut off our water,' Raf said, 'so our crops grow poorly and we Northmen become weaker and more susceptible to the illness. I came here only to—'

'*Silence!*' the king boomed, his voice ringing through the enormous hall. The assembled trolls quailed. The jesters literally cowered.

But Raf stood his ground.

The king's eyes bulged. 'Impudent thief! How dare you address me so! I have a good mind to snap one of your arms off right now and eat your bones in front of you! Northmen! *Northmen!* I know this tribe. A dirty rabble. They sent elders to bargain with me months ago. I received those old men on my winter throne. They, er, fell before me.'

The trolls near Raf sniggered.

The king boomed, 'Then these same *Northmen* sent a delegation of three young princes several weeks ago, princes who arrived with three porters. The lead prince, Bader was his name, offered me his porters in return for a small bottle of the Elixir.'

Raf's eyes widened in surprise.

The king saw it.

'Yes. Your prince offered *his own people* as payment for a sample of the Elixir. He did not ask for water or food or even a barrel of the magic drink. Just a single small bottle.'

Raf saw the scene in his mind. Bader had come here not to save the *tribe* from the illness at all. He had only come to save his own sister. And he had brought along the three porters not as assistants but as unsuspecting sacrificial offerings.

The king leered at Raf, his huge troll mouth salivating. 'I saw little honour in this Northman prince named Bader so I ate his porters anyway and threw him and his fellow princes in my cells to contemplate their treachery.'

Raf said nothing.

The king's eyes narrowed. 'But you, thief, you are not like him. You came here alone, under the cover of night, and you scaled an entire mountain to steal my Elixir. Were it not for my own precautions, you might have succeeded. No, you are motivated by a far more dangerous emotion than your prince was: the desire to save others. You . . . are a hero.'

The king raised his chin. 'Trolls! Today, as you know, is a special day, the day of my son's wedding. And so, as a wedding gift, I will give this hero to my son, Turv'—the king nodded to the tall red-robed troll at his right hand, who, Raf noted, also wore a grim fingerbone necklace plus a bone-sword at his waist made from a human leg—'as his matrimonial meal. While not as succulent as the meat of a child or a woman, the tough sinew of a hero will bring Turv that hero's strength.'

The crowd of trolls gasped and then applauded vigorously. This was an astonishing gift: captured enemy warriors were usually eaten only by the king himself.

'Tonight,' the king announced, 'at the wedding banquet for Turv and his bride, Graia, this thief will be ritually killed and his bones served bloody and fresh to Turv! Until then, put him in the cage, so I may look upon him throughout the day!'

Raf was led to a small iron cage that hung from a great chain. He was locked inside it and hoisted aloft, high above the floor of the hall for all to see: the live prisoner who would become that evening's celebratory meal.

For the remainder of that day, Raf sat forlornly in his cage, watching the trolls prepare for the evening's feast.

Draggers hauled great stone sleds into the hall from a side door on the eastern side. On those sleds were baskets of food, and jugs of water and mead.

While the draggers toiled, the king and his courtiers drank and laughed. By mid-afternoon, some had already passed out on the floor. At one point, the two little hobgoblin jesters drew laughs from the king's cronies by throwing fruit at Raf.

Shortly after that, Raf saw the bride and her mother enter the hall. The bride's mother was a big heavy-boned she-troll dressed in the kind of brown sack-cloth that seemed to be worn by most of the troll women. She walked with a purposeful stride and ignored the catcalls from the drunken males up near the throne.

The bride beside her could not have been more different from her mother. She was smaller and walked with a shy hunch, and she wore a sack-cloth that was far whiter than those worn by the other she-trolls. The unruly trolls nudged and elbowed Turv at the sight of her, behaving—it seemed to Raf—like immature boys.

And then it struck Raf: this she-troll was Graia, the she-troll Düm had beseeched the troll prince Turv not to marry.

Having witnessed the way troll society operated, Raf could see now what an outrageous thing Düm's approach to Turv had been: a lowly dragger questioning a prince.

Outrageous, but also brave. Düm might have been slow-witted, but he must have known such an approach was loaded with peril.

*

Late in the afternoon a commotion arose at the side door to the hall.

A crowd of trolls gathered there started oohing and ahing.

Raf looked that way—

—to see a pair of figures emerge from the throng of trolls and approach the king's throne.

Raf gripped the bars of his cage as his eyes went wide.

It was Düm and Ko.

And Düm was leading Ko by a rope, as his prisoner.

Düm yanked Ko into the Great Hall like a stubborn dog on a leash. Ko's beautiful gold rope was tied around the hermit's throat and the old man's hands were bound.

Ko tripped as Düm tugged on the rope, dragging him forward.

Düm called loudly: 'Trolls! I Düm! Recently, I flee from Troll Mountain after refusing challenge from Prince Turv! Now I come back, humbly seeking audience with king to present this captive as payment for my return to tribe!'

Up on the throne, the king and his rogues all turned, smirking but curious.

The prince named Turv looked down upon Düm with particular disdain.

'Father,' Raf heard Turv whisper, 'this is the

dragger I told you about.'

The king turned. 'The one who opposed your marriage to Graia?'

'The very same.'

Raf was confused. Had Düm turned on Ko? It seemed very unlikely. Or perhaps this was something else—

'Speak, dragger!' the king said imperiously.

Düm swallowed, clearly nervous to be addressing the king.

'Düm find this hermit in Badlands, sire.' Düm pulled up a stone sled behind him. On it were six small green barrels—the same barrels Raf had seen in Ko's hovel in the swamp: with 火粉末 written on them and candlewicks sticking out of their lids.

'Düm also find these barrels in old man's hut: barrels filled with dark salt.'

The crowd murmured. Salt was a greatly prized delicacy in these parts. To have salt on one's food was a privilege reserved only for the elite and even then, only when it was available— and here was Düm offering the king six barrels of the stuff.

But as Raf knew, those barrels did not contain salt . . .

And for the briefest of moments, Raf felt a flutter of hope. Düm was carrying out a plan.

Düm said stiffly, 'Düm bring barrels to king as extra payment for his crime, in hope that gift will absolve Düm of his insult to Prince Turv. But Düm know his fate rest in king's hands.'

Düm bowed his head.

The king pondered him for a long moment, his mean eyes calculating.

He said, 'To decline a challenge is the gravest crime in our society, dragger. It is not something I forgive lightly. However, I can see, with these gifts, you have gone to some trouble to make amends.' He looked at the crowd. 'As it is my son's wedding day and the insult was made against him, I shall let Prince Turv decide your fate. Turv? Do you seek to enforce your challenge against this dragger or do you accept his payment and release him from his obligation?'

Turv looked long and hard at Düm, then glanced at the watching crowd of trolls.

As the future king, Raf realised, the decision Turv made here was important. He could be seen as capricious and hard, or benevolent when the occasion called for it. That Düm had also brought the 'salt' barrels as an extra gift was clever—it made it very hard for Turv to turn him down.

In fact, Raf thought, it was actually *too* clever for Düm, and it made Raf wonder if this had not been Düm's plan at all . . .

'I accept both gifts and allow Düm back into the tribe,' Turv said in a loud voice.

The crowd of trolls nodded and clapped approvingly.

But then another voice cut the air.

Ko's voice.

'Your most wise and excellent majesty. May I speak?' the old man said in his polite way.

The king leaned back on his throne. 'Amuse me, human.'

'I have heard it said by trolls who wander in the Badlands that before you were *king*, you embraced the *challenge* of battles on the *Fighting Platform*.'

Raf frowned. Ko was putting unusual emphasis on certain words: *king, challenge, Fighting Platform*.

The king sat higher on his throne. 'You hear correctly. I was the previous king's champion, undefeated on the Fighting Platform.'

'Will there be any fights *during this wedding feast?*'

There it was again, Raf thought. The odd emphasis on certain words. The trolls didn't seem to notice it, but he did.

The king said, 'I imagine there will be, old man, especially if the mead is flowing. Why? Do you want to challenge somebody?'

The assembled trolls laughed loudly. The king enjoyed his own joke.

Ko smiled. 'Oh, no, no, your majesty. I only ask that *when you are done with your activities tonight, you release me.*'

Ko never looked at Raf as he spoke—not even a glance—but Raf now knew that Ko was addressing him and not the king.

Raf furrowed his brow, trying to figure out the meaning behind Ko's cryptic words: *king, challenge, Fighting Platform, during the wedding feast,* and *when you are done with your activities tonight, you release me.*

No . . . he thought.

It couldn't be . . .

Was Ko suggesting . . .

But that was madness.

Ignorant of the secret messages being passed, the king just laughed at Ko's words. 'Ha! Release you! My generosity only goes so far, old man. When this night is over, I will be sucking the marrow from your bones!'

Ko's eyes widened in surprise. 'Oh, dear . . .'

Turv stepped in. 'Guards. Take the old man to the cells on the western wall.' He turned to Düm: 'And you, dragger, take those salt barrels and ready them, we shall make use of them tonight. The whole tribe shall enjoy your gift. Then return to your duties: after all, we have a feast to prepare!'

Ko was taken away to the cells. Düm dragged his stone sled toward the kitchen area on the eastern side of the hall.

Raf was watching them both—still thinking about Ko's message—when, from his position in his suspended cage, he heard Turv say in a low voice to his lackeys: 'Later tonight, after I am wed, bring Düm to the Fighting Platform, unarmed. There I shall take my hammer to his knees until he begs me to end his life.'

The prince's cronies cackled.

Raf could only watch Düm dragging his sled toward the kitchen area, head bent, shoulders hunched, unaware that he had just been sentenced to die.

As the sun crept lower in the western sky and storm clouds moved in for the night, the trolls of Troll Mountain gathered in the Great Hall for the wedding of Prince Turv to the she-troll, Graia.

Throughout the afternoon, none of the trolls noticed Düm going about his labours—dragging sleds of food and positioning his prized barrels of salt around the hall. He placed them thus: one up on the king's podium, solely for the king's personal use; and three at the bases of three of the mighty columns of the hall (the fourth column, the north-eastern one, stood within the kitchen area and so didn't require one).

Raf, however, observed him every step of the way, and at one point, Düm risked a furtive glance up at Raf.

Then Düm went upstairs to the windswept Winter Throne Hall with the last two barrels and there—standing alone up on the magnificent open-air platform—he placed one barrel beside the king's winter throne. The sixth and final barrel he placed beside the north-western column of the Winter Throne Hall, for all the trolls to use. He also did one other thing.

Then, as the storm clouds took over the sky completely, night came, and the troll wedding began.

*

The Great Hall was abuzz with celebration.

Mead flowed, trolls danced, and the Troll King looked out over his minions and smiled. He threw back a goblet of frothing mead and belched loudly.

Then the wedding ceremony began and Turv and Graia stood on the steps of the king's podium, facing each other, Turv in his most princely attire and Graia dressed all in white, with wildflowers in her hair—an oddly sweet and delicate touch, Raf noticed, among such an indelicate race of creatures.

The she-troll looked miserable. Standing off to the side, so did Düm.

The king presided over the wedding ceremony.

'If any here should object to this union, let them say it now!' he called.

Silence answered him. No one—

'I have an objection!'

The crowd of trolls spun, searching for the objector. Their eyes rose as one.

It was Raf who had spoken.

King, challenge, Fighting Platform, during the wedding feast.

Raf swallowed deeply. He hoped he had interpreted Ko's cryptic message correctly.

'I object to being the celebratory meal for this foul occasion. King of the Trolls, I challenge *you* to combat on the Fighting Platform!'

*

The stir that followed Raf's words was unprecedented in troll history.

A human challenging a troll? Even more astounding, he was challenging the king! And as every troll knew, the king had a special privilege when it came to challenges—

'What did you say!' the king roared.

'I said, I challenge you, King of Fools, King

of *Nothing*!' Raf said defiantly, although on the inside his heart was pounding. This was what Ko had meant for him to do, wasn't it? 'Or do you *refuse* my challenge?'

The king's huge grey face reddened with rage. His tusks ground against each other.

'You challenge me? *You* challenge *me* . . . !'

Then the king's furious anger transformed into cool menace.

He nodded at his champion, the huge troll Grondo, as he spoke to Raf: 'You are not as clever as you think, thief. For while no troll may refuse a challenge, the king alone is accorded a singular privilege: if he be challenged, he can send his champion to fight on his behalf. We can't go having fools challenging the king anytime they want, now can we?'

Grondo stood to his full imposing height and the crowd started chanting, 'Grondo . . . Grondo . . .'

Even Turv, halfway through his own wedding ceremony, had a look of bloodlust in his eyes and he joined in the chant.

The king grinned nastily. 'Be careful what you wish for, thief. You want a fight, I'll give you a fight. Take him down! Let us all repair to the Winter Throne Hall and the Fighting Platform! After this thief is vanquished, we shall finish this ceremony and devour his flesh! To the Fighting Platform!'

The trolls poured up and out of the lone tunnel that granted access to the Winter Throne Hall, fanning out as they did so, rushing eagerly to the eastern side of the great open space so as to get the best view of the Fighting Platform.

Storm clouds rumbled overhead. Rain was coming.

The king and his entourage mounted the winter throne while Raf and Grondo marched across the open-air hall, through the ranks of trolls, to a plank-bridge leading to the Fighting Platform.

As Raf strode past all the trolls, they mocked him, spat at him, declared their eagerness to see his blood.

But then, fleetingly, Raf noticed two things:

first, he snatched a glimpse of one of Ko's distinctive little green barrels over by the north-western column. And second, he saw Düm.

The gentle troll was lingering at the very back of the crowd of trolls, over by the single entrance cut into the floor of the Winter Throne Hall, unnoticed by any of the others.

Before he could see any more of Düm, Raf was shoved across the plank-bridge onto the Fighting Platform. Grondo followed behind him.

The two hobgoblin jesters were already on the wooden stage, pantomiming a death match. One stabbed the other with an imaginary sword and the second one fell, clutching his chest in mock agony. The two jesters scampered off the platform as Raf and Grondo stepped onto it.

The plank was removed and Raf suddenly found himself standing alone with the troll champion out on the round wooden stage, high above the eastern slope of the mountain. The stage was perfectly circular, perhaps twenty feet across, and made of thick wooden planks.

By the gods, Raf thought, now he *really* hoped he had interpreted Ko correctly.

The sight of the barrel made him think that

perhaps he had, but then again, he might have got it all terribly, terribly wrong—

'Choose your weapons!' a troll who appeared to be some kind of referee called.

'My war hammer!' called Grondo.

The crowd cheered.

'And you, thief? Choose your weapon, for what it will be worth!'

The trolls laughed.

Raf thought for a moment. 'My axe.'

A massive hammer was thrown onto the platform. A troll was sent below to the cell area where Raf's axe had been sequestered.

As he waited for its delivery, Raf's eyes scanned the Fighting Platform desperately. He was sure Ko had been directing him to challenge the king, knowing that such a challenge could not be refused, and thus bring himself *here*—although perhaps Ko hadn't known about the king's special privilege. And Raf had seen the barrel up here, and Düm . . .

But *why*? What was Ko's plan? The Fighting Platform was completely bare. There was absolutely nothing here that Raf could use.

He looked up and saw that, owing to the way the platform extended out from the Winter

Throne Hall, he could see the crenellated battlement ringing the summit of Troll Mountain, complete with its troll-added horns.

If he could fling a rope over those horns, he supposed, his current position offered a viable route up to the Supreme Watchtower, but such a throw was well beyond his range and right now, with the imposing figure of Grondo looming before him, finding a rope and throwing it was the last thing he could do.

At that moment, Raf's axe was tossed onto the Fighting Platform and the scene was set.

The massed trolls leaned forward, leering, salivating. The Troll King grinned nastily. His son, Turv, did the same; his wedding day would be remembered for a long, long time.

Raf's heart sank.

He'd clearly got Ko's plan wrong, and now he would have to face the trolls' best fighter in mortal combat.

Grondo towered over him, impossibly huge, his tusks rising from hairy tufts on his jaws, one of his great grey fists gripping his enormous hammer.

Raf just stood there, puny and thin, holding his home-made double-bladed axe. The axe hardly looked capable of nicking Grondo's thick hide.

Then it started raining. Thick pelting drops. The trolls didn't even notice. Rain didn't bother trolls.

'We don't have to do this, you know,' Raf said to the champion. 'We don't have to fight.'

Grondo smirked. 'Fool. You do not realise. This fight has already begun.'

*

Grondo lunged.

Raf dived. And the hammer came down on the stage with a resounding boom. So powerful was the blow, splinters flew up from the slats.

Grondo swung again, chasing after Raf, but Raf dived clear again.

Boom, boom, boom!

Duck, roll, dive.

The rain kept pouring. Lightning flashed.

The crowd cheered at every swing.

*

As the trolls roared at the action on the Fighting Platform, at the very back of the crowd, Düm came alongside the she-troll, Graia.

159

'Graia,' he whispered. 'If you want to leave Troll Mountain forever, come with me now.'

Without a word, Graia took Düm's hand and followed him down the stairs, away from the Winter Throne Hall.

A short way down, in a tight bottleneck of a tunnel, with the echoes of the crowd far above them, Düm did a strange thing: he closed the thick stone door—the only point of entry or exit to the Winter Throne Hall—and then he reinforced it with a pair of heavy stone sleds parked nearby.

Almost the whole troll community was up on the winter hall watching the fight . . . and he had just trapped them all up there.

*

Somehow, Raf was still alive, dodging and evading Grondo's mighty swipes, slipping and sliding in the rain.

The rain didn't help Grondo's footwork and at one point, Raf managed to run under one of the big troll's lusty blows and swing at him with his little lightweight axe—and he drew blood from the troll!

The axe cut Grondo's skin under the armpit, in one of the few places where a troll's skin was soft and sensitive.

Grondo froze.

The crowd gasped.

The big champion touched the nick, and saw his own blood on his fingertip. He glared balefully at Raf.

He wasn't hurt. He was *angry*.

Grondo roared, a great bellow, and, raising his hammer above his head, came charging at Raf.

Hammer blows rained down around the darting figure of Raf and had any one of them hit, he would have been knocked senseless and done for.

Grondo's charge was fast and furious and relentless and it afforded Raf no chance of reply. Indeed, it took all his nimbleness to evade the flurry of blows—until suddenly, Grondo anticipated one of his moves and trapped him at the edge of the stage.

Grondo had him.

Raf had nowhere to go. He stood there exposed, soaked by the rain and lit by the lightning storm.

The big troll swung the final blow of this match and Raf went flailing off the edge of the platform.

Raf went cartwheeling over the edge of the stage.

To the massed crowd of trolls, it looked as if Grondo had dispatched him once and for all with the mighty blow, but both Raf and Grondo knew that Grondo had hit only air.

Out of sheer desperation, Raf had intentionally dived off the Fighting Platform, reaching for the edge with his hands while Grondo's hammer swished above him, missing him by inches—so that now Raf clung by his fingertips to the Fighting Platform's rain-spattered edge, his feet dangling high above the deadly drop.

But Grondo knew it wasn't over.

The big champion stomped forward to see where his opponent had gone, but as he did so, Raf swung himself *underneath* the platform, gripping his axe handle in his teeth while clutching the network of rafters under the platform with his hands, disappearing completely from every troll's sight!

After a couple of swings, Raf stopped suddenly. He saw something wedged between two of the support beams. Something that must have been left here by . . .

He *had* interpreted Ko correctly.

Raf swung forward with renewed energy.

*

Up on the Winter Throne Hall, the crowd of trolls grunted and murmured in astonishment. None of them had ever seen this happen before.

Grondo dropped to all fours and peered out over the edge of the platform, when abruptly, Raf's head appeared at the opposite edge behind him.

'Over there!' the trolls called.

Grondo spun and moving with frightening speed, bounded over to where Raf was trying to climb back up onto the stage, grabbing his axe from between his teeth with his free hand—

—but Grondo was on him too quickly, and he seized the axe from Raf's hand, wrenching it away—

—only to reveal a knife still in Raf's hand, the flint knife he kept concealed in the axe's handle, and with a quick but firm thrust, Raf plunged the knife deep into the soft flesh on the underside of Grondo's chin.

Grondo froze, his eyes wide—the knife had gone right up into his brain.

There was a flash of lightning.

The assembled trolls fell silent. Even the jesters stood motionless in astonishment.

The drumming of the rain was the only sound.

Then Grondo fell.

His rigid body toppled forward, falling clear over Raf, and he dropped off the Fighting Platform, sailing down, down, down through the air above the eastern side of the mountain before he smashed against the rocks far below, his body spraying blood in every direction. But Grondo had been dead long before he struck the rocks.

The crowd of trolls remained silent, thunderstruck.

This was unheard of.

But what happened next was unthinkable.

*

Reaching underneath the platform, Raf brought up the object he had spied wedged between the support beams earlier.

Ko's crossbow.

Tied to it was Ko's beautiful gold-coloured rope.

Before the trolls even knew what he was doing, Raf raised the crossbow and fired it—not at any of them—but upward, at one of the big horns extending out from the battlement crowning the summit of the mountain.

Given the Fighting Platform's slight protuberance from the Winter Throne Hall, he had a clear shot.

This was Ko's plan: to complete his mission, Raf had needed to get to the Fighting Platform, where he would find the crossbow—planted there by Düm—and use it to get up to the Supreme Watchtower and get the Elixir.

After that, somehow, he had to get back down.

An arrow shot out of the crossbow with terrific force, soaring up through the rain-streaked air, trailing the rope behind it like a wobbling tail, before it looped over the horn at the north-eastern corner of the battlement and held.

Then Raf did the most outrageous thing of all.

He slung the crossbow over his shoulder, gripped the gold-threaded rope, and, pelted by the rain, took a fast-running leap out to the north of the Fighting Platform and . . .

. . . swung . . .

. . . in a long swooping arc out, around and behind the king's winter throne, high above the rear flank of Troll Mountain.

His daring swing ended in the space behind the king's podium, far from any of the trolls massed near the Fighting Platform.

And before any of them had even started to move from their places near the Fighting Platform, Raf was climbing, nimbly and quickly, hand over hand, up the now-vertical rope, heading for the summit of Troll Mountain for the second time.

The race was on. Only now it was Raf versus the entire population of Troll Mountain.

Raf surmounted the battlement and scanned the area fearfully.

There were no guards up here—they had all gone downstairs, either for the feast or the fight.

Raf dashed inside a thick stone doorway and found the set of spiralling internal stairs that led up to the Supreme Watchtower. (He knew these stairs—he had been marched down them when he had been captured. The spiralling stone stairwell led both up to the watchtower and down to a narrower set of spiral stairs hidden within the north-western column of the Winter Throne Hall.)

As he pounded up the stairwell, Raf heard shouts from below: 'He's up in the watchtower!' 'Cover the battlement!'

The trolls were coming.

Raf kept running determinedly upward, his face fixed.

Raf came to the ladder leading to the topmost section of the Supreme Watchtower, clambered up it and burst into Vilnar's laboratory, warm and candlelit, with its vast collection of jars, barrels and foodstuffs.

He saw Vilnar, rising sleepily from a straw mat on the floor.

'You? Again?'

'Vilnar! Come with me now if you want to escape your confinement!'

'Escape—?'

'Now or not at all!'

The little troll grabbed a small sack of food. 'Now it is.'

'I also need these.' Raf moved to the side work-bench and grabbed the three small glass bottles with the amber Elixir in them. He wrapped them in rags then put the rags in a pouch which he slung from his waist.

He had his prize.

Now he had to get out of here.

Vilnar came alongside him as they strode back toward the ladder. 'Your determination is impressive, but determination alone isn't enough. What is your plan now? They will cover the battlement and then storm this tower.'

'I'm actually following someone else's plan,' Raf said. 'I'm just trying to figure out what it is.'

*

The trolls were in a state of shock and bewilderment.

First the death of Grondo. Then the human's incredible swing off the Fighting Platform and his nimble climb to the summit of Troll Mountain.

He had been caught trying to steal their Elixir . . . and now he was trying to steal it *again*, right in front of them all!

'Guards!' the king roared. 'Get him or I shall dine on *you* tonight!'

The guard-trolls burst into action.

A dozen of them threw open the secret door to the stairwell inside the north-western column and started up its internal stairs.

Six of them left the stairwell to cover the battlement while the other six continued up the spiralling stairs toward the watchtower . . .

. . . only to hear an ominous booming noise

coming from somewhere higher up the stone stairwell.

Boom!

Boom!

Boom!

The guard-trolls swapped confused glances. What was this?

The great booms became louder and faster before suddenly seven large wooden barrels came tumbling out of the upper reaches of the stairwell at speed, rampaging down the steps, careening off the spiralling walls.

The first barrel slammed into the first troll with frightening force and swept him clean off his feet, hurling the big troll backward before bouncing further down the stairs, past the other shocked guards.

The guards managed to dodge and duck the rain of heavy barrels that followed, but not without injury. The tumbling rush of barrels crashed and careered past them, bouncing down the stairs into the darkness below.

The guards pressed on upward and entered the watchtower with their hammers raised . . .

. . . and found it empty.

No thief. No wise old troll either.

The guards rushed down to the battlement to ask the six guards there if the fugitives had come down that way, only to be told that they had not.

The guard-trolls looked at each other, bamboozled.

*

In the meantime, some of the other trolls had headed for the door leading back down to the Great Hall, only to find it closed and barricaded from the other side.

The Troll King, on his winter throne, looked about in confusion and rage.

*

At the base of the stairwell hidden inside the north-western column of the Winter Throne Hall, the last of the seven barrels thrown from the watch-tower bounced to a halt.

Its lid was kicked open from within, and out of it, wrapped in a padding of cloth and hay, popped Raf.

The barrel beside him wobbled and Raf heard a muffled shout from inside it. He ripped off its lid and pulled out Vilnar.

'This way,' Raf said grimly, pulling Vilnar by the hand.

As they dashed for the door, Raf pulled one of Ko's bulbous flint-tipped arrows from a clip on the side of the crossbow and struck it against the stone wall, igniting it in a flash of flame.

*

Raf and Vilnar emerged from the north-western column at a run. The trolls near the king's throne saw them immediately and took off in pursuit.

But, just before he raced out into the rain-storm, Raf dashed past the small green barrel set up beside the great column—and as he did so, without missing a step, he touched his flaming arrowhead to the barrel's candlewick.

The wick ignited like a fuse . . .

Raf saw the trolls massing over by the stopped-up exit to the Winter Throne Hall—and figured that Düm had been there, too—and in that same moment, he also realised that Ko had even suggested his escape route.

'We can't get down!' Vilnar yelled.

'Yes we can!'

Chased by the horde of trolls, Raf bolted for

the *western* side of the Winter Throne Hall. No rail protected its edge. Mountains loomed beyond it, veiled in rain. Empty air fell away before him and Vilnar.

'Grab hold of me!' Raf yelled as they came to the edge.

Vilnar gripped his waist while Raf pulled out his crossbow and, at the very moment that the sizzling fuse on the firepowder barrel beside the north-western column burned down to its base and the little barrel exploded violently—*obliterating* the column, transforming it in a single shattering instant into a cloud of stone dust—Raf launched the two of them off the edge of the mountaintop!

*

As Raf and Vilnar leaped off the western edge of the Winter Throne Hall, a shocking scene occurred behind them.

The blast of the firepowder barrel had completely destroyed the north-western column, thus causing the entire roof of the Winter Throne Hall *and the whole summit of the mountain above it* to come crashing down on the rear half of the open-air space.

With a momentous boom, the mountain's summit slammed down onto the Winter Throne Hall and toppled clear *off* its rear northern edge, where it fell for two thousand feet before splashing into the dam-lake that curled around the rear of Troll Mountain, sending a stupendous gout of white water spraying into the air.

The rearward angle of the summit's fall meant that none of the two hundred trolls trying to flee the open-air hall were killed or even hurt, but those few guards who were still inside the summit screamed all the way down.

While this was happening, Raf slid down the rain-slicked surface of the upper western flank of Troll Mountain, bouncing on his backside with Vilnar still clinging to him.

After about a hundred feet of sliding, they sailed off a second brink and, for a moment, found themselves *two thousand dizzying feet* above the stakes at the bottom of the mountain's vertical western face—the same stakes that lay beneath the triangular prison cells cut into that flank.

As he and Vilnar flew out into thin air, Raf reached out with his crossbow and hooked it around the roof of the small shack that housed the elevator mechanism servicing the cells.

The crossbow snagged the edge of the roof . . .

. . . and Raf and Vilnar suddenly swung inward and landed in an ungainly heap on the wooden platform directly underneath the shack—the platform with the hole in its floor through which the elevator was raised and lowered.

Dazed, Raf shook his head and looked up to see the huge shadow of a troll standing right in front of him!

Before Raf could move, the troll had lifted him bodily into the air, gripping him firmly in its massive hands, drawing him up to its huge grey face.

A face that Raf recognised.

It was Düm.

*

'Master Raf, you are crazy human, but you smart, you figure out Master Ko's plan. Düm hope you pleased with Düm's efforts. It very hard for Düm to remember all of Master Ko's instructions.'

'You've been great, Düm,' Raf said. 'Thank you.'

It was then that Raf noticed Graia standing behind the troll. 'You must be Graia.'

'I am. And I am coming with you.'

'I'm pleased to hear it,' Raf said. He could hear the loud banging of the trolls trying to break down the upper door that Düm had barricaded.

'We're not out of this yet. We have an old man to rescue and then we have to run as fast as we can. Düm, the wheel, please.'

*

Within minutes, with Düm turning the great cogwheel that raised and lowered the elevator and Raf standing on the elevator itself, they found Ko in his cliff-side cell.

The old man was very pleased to see Raf. He stepped onto the elevator.

'You listen well, my young friend,' Ko said as Düm raised them up. 'And I am most glad you came back for me on your way out.'

'You did ask me to,' Raf said. 'Although did you really expect me to beat the trolls' champion in single combat?'

Ko shrugged. 'I told you before: a quest would not be a quest if it were easy. Either you beat their champion or you failed in your mission—'

Pained cries interrupted him.

The other prisoners—most of them starving

Southmen and Southwomen—had seen them on the elevator and were desperately begging to be rescued, too.

Raf was momentarily taken aback.

Apart from his spontaneous decision to free Vilnar, he hadn't thought of rescuing anyone else. He had come to Troll Mountain for the Elixir and he had only stopped here to grab Ko on the way out.

Then another voice called, 'Raf! Raf!'

Raf turned.

It was Bader. He was standing with his legs astride his inverted triangular hole, peering up and out at Raf.

'Take me with you,' Bader croaked. 'Please.'

Raf stared at him, at this pale imitation of the formerly haughty prince.

'I have the Elixir, Bader.' He indicated the pouch hanging from his hip. 'I can save our tribe.'

'Please take me with you, Raf.'

And in Bader's desperation, Raf saw something. Bader was just as desperate to live as the Southmen prisoners were.

In that moment, Raf knew that whether they be Northmen or Southmen, they were all the same, they were all people, and if he saved one of these captives now, he had to save them all.

'People, listen to mc! If you want to flee this place, get on this contraption now! This is your one and only chance of escape!'

And so, hauled up by the mighty exertions of Düm, the great escape from the cliff-side cells of the trolls began.

It took four trips to release all fifteen prisoners—first Ko and Bader plus one other man; then all of the others in groups of four.

Raf would greet each load of prisoners at the elevator platform and send them on their way with the words, 'Go! Don't look back!'

Bader had not needed a second invitation. He stole away immediately, dashing inside the mountain while Raf stayed at the elevator platform to release the other captives.

The bangs of the trolls on the upper stone door continued and just as Raf helped the last prisoner—a young woman from the Southmen tribe—from the elevator, he heard a great rending crack and then troll voices shouting angrily.

'They've broken through Düm's barricade,' he said to Ko. 'We have to go!'

Running at the rear of the group of fleeing captives, Raf, Ko, Vilnar, Düm, and Graia dashed back down to the Great Hall of the Mountain King.

The noise of the trolls rampaging down the stairways and tunnels behind them rang in their ears.

It was now a race to get out.

Hurrying last of all, Raf came to the top of the spiral stairs circling the outer flank of one of the pillars of the Great Hall. Looking behind him, he saw the shadows of the pursuing trolls coming around the corner of the tunnel, heard the thunder of their footsteps.

As he started down the stairs, emerging near the ceiling of the Great Hall, he touched his waist to check that he still had the pouch containing the Elixir—

He felt no pouch.

Raf looked at his waist.

The pouch was gone.

'What in the name of—' Had he dropped it? Had—

'Raf! Hurry!' Ko called back.

'I've lost the Elix—'

And then Raf saw him.

He looked out across the hall just in time to see Bader dash out through the huge main doorway.

Gripped tightly in Bader's hand was Raf's pouch.

*

Raf's eyes almost popped out of his head.

Bader! He must have lifted it from my belt when I was busy freeing the other captives.

His anger was short-lived, for just then, with a terrifying bellow, the first furious troll appeared at the top of the spiral stairs only ten steps away from Raf.

Raf flew down the stone stairs—leaping down them three at a time as the upper reaches of the spiralling stairway filled with more and more trolls.

Having broken through the barricaded door up top, now the full horde of two hundred angry trolls flooded down *all four* of the stair-ringed pillars of the Great Hall!

It was a fearsome and spectacular sight: the mass of trolls looked like a swarm of ants streaming down the four spiralling staircases, trying to head off the fleeing captives, especially the one they thought was stealing their Elixir.

The Southmen captives raced out the main door after Bader but well behind him. They burst out into the stormy night and hurried down the steep royal staircase, heading for the Main Gate at its base. The door and staircase which had once been reserved for troll royalty were now being used as the main route of escape by the fleeing captives.

Raf hit the floor of the hall at a run and saw that all four pillars were now teeming with trolls. He joined Ko at the main door as Düm, Graia, and Vilnar ran out into the rainstorm, heading down the royal stairway.

'Raf!' Ko called. 'The barrels! Shoot the barrels!'

Raf turned and saw them: Ko's three *other* fire-powder barrels arrayed around the Great Hall, at the bases of three of the four pillars, the same barrels he had seen Düm placing earlier.

But then, in a fleeting instant, another thought struck Raf: something bigger than his own escape or that of the other prisoners.

To Ko's surprise, Raf took off, running back into the Great Hall of the Mountain King, but off to the right, to the eastern side, heading for the nearest pillar on that side.

'What are you doing!' Ko called. 'Use the flaming arrows to ignite the barrels!'

'Go!' Raf yelled back. 'Get out of here!'

'But Raf—'

'Remember your own lesson: to bring down a four-legged creature, I only need to disable two of its legs. Now go!'

Ko just shook his head and raced out the main door, leaving Raf to his madness.

*

As he ran, Raf extracted a flaming arrowhead, struck it against the floor, igniting it, and notched it in his crossbow.

Then with the ranks of trolls streaming down toward him, he fired the flaming arrow diagonally across the width of the hall.

The arrow streaked across the wide interior space and slammed into the green barrel at the base of the north-western pillar, penetrating it with its flaming head.

The barrel exploded.

A moment later, the immense pillar, cracked at its base, toppled. All the trolls on it fell every which way, flung clear.

The mountain trembled.

But the hall was still intact.

Raf reached the pillar he had been running toward—the south-eastern one—and scooped up the small firepowder barrel at its base.

The trolls on this pillar, led by the king and Prince Turv, were almost down its stairs, practically right on top of Raf.

Ignoring their pounding footfalls and their furious roars, Raf calmly armed his crossbow with another flaming arrowhead, levelled the crossbow at the opposite pillar—the south-western one—and fired.

Again, the arrow streaked across the hall and

lodged in the barrel just as the first troll leaped off that pillar's stairway and started running across the hall toward Raf.

The barrel exploded.

With a great rending crash, that pillar crumbled, too, sending trolls sailing off it, tumbling to the floor.

And now the ceiling of the Great Hall began to crack. Enormous chunks of stone began to drop down from it. With two of its supporting pillars now crippled, the weight of the ceiling could no longer be upheld.

And as Raf raced out the door in the eastern wall with the barrel under his arm and dashed down the dragging ramp there, the magnificent ceiling of the Great Hall of the Mountain King came crashing down on the mass of trolls, crushing them in a thunderous and devastating avalanche of stone.

The Hall of the Mountain King was no more.

*

But it wasn't over yet.

Troll Mountain itself was collapsing.

With the hall at its heart imploding, *the entire mountain* now began to fall.

For Raf's arrow shots had not been random: since he had destroyed the pillars on the *western* side of the hall, the mountain now toppled in that direction.

Backlit by lightning and veiled by rain, with a great crashing noise, the top half of Troll Mountain—having already lost its summit—tilted westward, breaking away from its base, folding at the waist like a slow-falling tree. As the mountain crumbled, it turned boulders to dust and sent a great cloud of that dust billowing outward.

The whole great mountain then disappeared inside its own dust cloud as it smashed down against the nearest mountain to the west.

Ko, Vilnar, Düm, and Graia only barely managed to outrun the toppling peak. As it fell westward, it took the top half of the royal staircase with it, but fortunately for them, they had just hurried past the point where the staircase was violently ripped away.

It was likewise for Raf.

Safe on the eastern flank of the mountain, with the last little green barrel held under his arm, he just watched the great mountain peak break off from its base and fall away from him.

He found himself at the top of the dragging ramp, near a couple of stone sleds.

It was raining so hard that a small stream of water now flowed down the path as if it were a broad gutter.

Raf thought about using one of the sleds to slide down the sloping ramp, but figured he'd never be able to move one into position, so he just started running down the slick wet path.

He hadn't taken twenty steps when a furious shout from behind made him spin.

The Troll King stood above him, covered head to toe in stone dust, his tusked face twisted with rage, his eyes red with fury.

'You!' he cried.

The pouring rain quickly mixed with the layer of dust on his huge body, turning it into streaking rivulets of mud that looked like grim war paint.

The king also spied the sleds and, one-handed, hurled one onto the dragging ramp. He leaped onto it, then pushed it hard so that it began to slide toward Raf down the rain-slicked stone path.

Raf saw two choices: be crushed under the weight of the heavy stone sled or dive off the outer edge of the path to avoid the sled and die that way.

The sled came rushing toward him, picking up speed. Through years of daily use, the Dragging Path was worn smooth. In this storm, with the added lubricant of the stream flowing down it, the path became a slick trench that could convey a sled at great speed.

The sled rushed toward Raf, aided by the water, but instead of going under it or diving clear of it, Raf did something else: he leaped up and *onto* the speeding sled—still gripping his green barrel—crashing into the Troll King and, thanks to the extra weight of the barrel, knocking the big troll onto his backside.

Now they were *both* on the sled and the sled was still speeding down the path.

Raf hauled himself off the Troll King, just in time to avoid a lashing blow from the angry troll.

Raf regathered his footing as the sled swept around the curve of the Dragging Path, rushing toward the Main Gate.

As it came round the base of the mountain—with the upper half of the mountain still collapsing and boulders bouncing down the mountainside and rain pouring and lightning flashing—Raf saw the end of the path come into view.

The path opened onto a small wooden loading enclosure built beneath the solid stone bridge of the Main Gate. Beyond the slats of the little loading enclosure was nothing but a vertical drop into the deep ravine beneath the Main Gate.

If they didn't slow down soon, Raf saw, he and the Troll King would go blasting right through those puny wooden slats.

The king swung at Raf. Raf ducked the blow, standing with surprising balance on the speeding sled, balance that the troll didn't have.

The sled careened down the slope.

The Troll King grew angrier. He swung again, but Raf dived past him and just as the sled whipped under the bridge at the base of the path, Raf scooped up his barrel and leaped skyward, as high as he could, his free arm outstretched, and he gripped an overhanging rafter of the bridge one-handed while the king and the sled shot onward, blasting through the wooden slats of the loading enclosure as if they were twigs and out into the air above the ravine.

Raf's legs swung high, but he managed to hold on just long enough to fall in a clumsy heap on the path, its flowing stream coursing over his body.

His last memory of the cruel Troll King was an image of the big troll's mud-painted face disappearing into the darkness, awash with shock and incomprehension at his defeat. He fell into darkness, falling with the rain, never to be seen again.

*

Exhausted, bleeding, and soaked to the bone, Raf climbed some nearby stairs to join Düm and Ko at the Main Gate.

He found them—with Vilnar, Graia, and the Southmen captives—standing forlornly at the Main Gate's outer door, looking out at the space where the watchtower's long rope-bridge had once hung.

Raf saw the cause of their dismay.

The rope-bridge now dangled vertically and uselessly from the stanchions on their side of the chasm.

'It was that fellow from your tribe,' Ko said. 'He cut the bridge behind him after he got across.'

'Bader . . .' Raf breathed, also thinking of the Elixir Bader had stolen. By cutting the bridge, he must have thought he had condemned Raf to capture and death at the hands of the trolls while he would return in triumph to the tribe.

The rain kept falling on Raf and his group as they beheld their sorry plight.

Raf, however, turned away. 'It is no matter. I didn't intend to leave this way anyway. There's one more thing to be done.'

With the ruined hulk of Troll Mountain towering above him—half as tall as it used to be—Raf hurried down the lower Dragging Path to the rocky dam at the mountain's base.

There he placed the last green barrel of firepowder halfway up the dam's face and lit the fuse.

Moments later, after he had scurried off the ungainly pile of boulders, a great explosion sprayed out from the face of the dam. Rocky chunks went flying outward and then—

—an immense body of water surged through the newly created hole in the dam, rushing through it with awesome force, breaking down the rest of the ugly structure with ease before flowing in a mighty wave down the dry muddy waterway that led out of the Black Mountains.

Raf smiled grimly.

The river had been reborn.

With the trolls vanquished, crushed in their own lair, and the Elixir obtained—if not in the manner Raf had intended—Raf set about returning home.

As the river settled into a more regular flow, he and the others dismantled the trolls' wooden dock by the dam and set about crafting several broad rafts from its slats.

As they went about their work, Raf conversed with several members of the Southmen tribe and he found them to be fair and decent folk—which was totally contrary to everything he had been told about the Southmen.

Raf pondered this.

So many of the things he had been told had turned out not to be true—the nature of the land to the north of the mountains, the general rogu-ishness of the Southmen. It made him wonder if people accept what they are told too quickly.

In any case, after a time the rafts were com-pleted and soon Raf and the group were sailing down the wide free-flowing river out of the land of the trolls.

*

In the Badlands, the river had reclaimed the muddy bogs and swamps, and at one stage in their journey back, Raf saw the place where he and Ko had met Düm for the first time—only now the gripping mud beneath the Broken Bridge was completely submerged by the river and was no longer a danger.

Although he was keen to return to Kira, Raf stopped at Ko's shack. There, Ko and the three trolls, Düm, Graia, and Vilnar, stepped off their rafts.

'Thank you both for everything,' Raf said to Düm and Ko. 'I would be inside the Troll King's belly now were it not for your cunning plan, Ko, and your clever following of it, Düm.'

Ko nodded. 'It was my pleasure. I always thought there was something in you, Raf, but your bravery is greater than even I imagined. I hope your sister recovers and you both live long and fulfilling lives.'

'I should also return this to you.' Raf offered Ko his crossbow.

'Keep it,' Ko said. 'Take it apart and see how it works, and then perhaps build your own version.'

Vilnar stepped forward and took Raf's hand. 'And let *me* thank *you*, young man. You had no obligation to free me and take me with you, but you did. I shall forever be in your debt.'

'Where will you go from here?' Raf asked.

'I will stay with Ko for a while. It will be quite nice to discuss philosophy with an equal mind. Then I plan to head back to the plains I once called home. You know what they say, once a field troll, always a field troll. It will be wonderful to live under the wide blue sky again—that is the gift you have given me.'

Finally, Raf turned to face Düm. 'And what will become of you now, my big friend?'

Düm took Raf's hand in his own giant grey paw. 'Strange, but Düm not sad to see trolls finished. Troll society cruel. Now Graia and Düm last trolls left in these parts. Think we head north, to find nice cold place to live in peace, away from humans. Not all humans as nice as Master Raf and may not like trolls living nearby. Thank you again for saving Düm's life.'

'I think we can safely say that you have repaid your debt to me.' Raf smiled and Düm gave him a sudden hug that almost crushed him.

'It's time I returned to my tribe,' Raf said, looking away toward his valley.

Ko gave Raf an odd smile. 'You have achieved much, young Raf, and you have learned much, too, but I fear there is one more lesson for you to learn and it will be a hard one.'

'What do you mean?'

'I have actually told you already,' Ko said. 'But I cannot tell you again. This you must discover for yourself.'

Raf nodded warily. 'Goodbye, Ko.'

'Goodbye, Raf. It has been my pleasure to assist you in your noble quest. Now, go and live.'

And so Raf returned to his raft and sailed down the reborn river.

As he did so, he drifted into a reverie. Images from his adventure flashed across his mind: fighting his way through the kingdom of the hobgoblins; swinging hand over hand across the rope-bridge to get to Troll Mountain; battling Grondo on the Fighting Platform.

He also remembered some comments he had heard over the course of his quest. The first was from Vilnar in the Supreme Watchtower:

'*Young man, pay attention! The illness, it is not a curse or an omen or black magic. It comes from a lack of nutrients—nutrients peculiar to lemons, oranges, and limes. That is all. Which means the Elixir is not magical either, it is merely a juice made from those same fruits.'*

And Ko: *'When you go in search of elixirs, be sure you know exactly what an elixir is.'*

As his raft meandered down the river, Raf thought about these comments a lot.

At length, he came to the top of his valley and there he parted ways with the Southmen.

Before the Southmen took their leave of him, however, Raf gave them one final gift. He told them how to cure the disease. They could do this, he said, simply by drinking the juices of lemons, oranges, or limes.

The Southmen thanked him profusely for this knowledge and promised that his name would long be remembered by them. Then they continued their journey on foot, returning to their own lands via a path that went around the domain of the Northmen. While they respected Raf, they felt that the other Northmen might not take kindly to Southmen sailing right through the middle of their lands.

And so Raf travelled the rest of the way alone.

After a time, he arrived back in the territory of the Northmen and stepped ashore. He gathered some lemons from a nearby grove and headed for the village.

Emerging from the woods, he stopped short.

Night had fallen and he saw the glow of many fires up ahead, coming from the centre of the village. He heard the sounds of fast-paced drums and joyful singing.

Putting that out of his mind for the moment, he hurried to his hovel and there he found Kira, alone in her straw bed, sweating and in a tormented sleep. He woke her gently and, squeezing his newfound lemons, fed her their juice. She became a little calmer, rejoiced briefly at his safe return, and then resumed her sleep. Raf didn't expect the juice—the Elixir—to work immediately, but he sensed even then that her healing had begun.

Only then did he turn his mind to the sounds of drums and singing. Leaving his weapons—his knife and his crossbow—in the hovel, he headed off in the direction of the central square.

*

Dirty, bloody, bruised, and bedraggled, Raf stepped out into the firelight and beheld a scene of great celebration and happiness.

The tribe was dancing and singing around a blazing fire.

Seated on a wooden throne at the head of the celebrations—not unlike the Troll King in his hall—was the chief of the tribe, and beside him, Bader, looking exceptionally proud, with his three bottles of the prized Elixir dangling from a strap around his neck.

The king's daughter, Lilibala, sat with them, occasionally reaching over to take a privileged sip of Elixir from one of the bottles hanging from her brother's neck. The wide-eyed boy named Timbuk served Bader with awestruck deference.

Every few moments, one of the girls of the tribe would rush up to Bader and steal a kiss on his cheek. He would smile indulgently: he was the hero who had returned with the precious medicine and he could have his pick of them.

And that was all Raf could bear.

'Quiet!' he called over the din. 'Quiet! All of you!'

The drums fell silent. The dancing stopped. All eyes turned to him.

The fat chief said, 'Why, if it isn't—'

'Be silent, you,' Raf commanded and the townsfolk gasped.

The chief's eyes went wide with anger. No one in the tribe had ever spoken to him so impudently.

Bader was less shocked. He eyed Raf coolly.

'Raf. I am so pleased you have returned from your journey. I do not know where you went, but much has happened in your absence. I confronted the trolls, destroyed their kingdom, and returned with their Elixir. Our tribe is saved and I am their hero. The Northmen are free of the tyranny of the trolls *and* the disease that has so terribly afflicted us. Oh, and as the heir to our illustrious chief's throne, I will cut out your tongue if you speak to my father in such a tone again.'

'Bader, you could no more cut out my tongue than fly over the mountains,' Raf said, and the assembled tribesfolk gasped again. 'We were *both* at the kingdom of the trolls and it was I who attained the Elixir. You stole it from me and fled ahead of me.'

Bader laughed. 'Honestly, Raf. Do you expect anyone here to believe that? I am a warrior. You are a runt. Do you think anyone here cannot recall our wrestling match at last year's harvest games? Who do you think is more likely to better the trolls, you or me?'

'How is the Elixir made, Bader?' Raf asked suddenly. 'Do you know that?'

Bader frowned, surprised, unsure how to respond.

'What will you do when those bottles of Elixir run dry?' Raf pressed. 'I, however, know what the Elixir is made of. I can make more of it.'

At this, the assembled crowd began to swap glances and murmur.

Bader noticed this and regathered himself. He raised his voice, more for the crowd than for Raf. 'Enough of this nonsense! We are celebrating!' He turned to his fellow warriors. 'My brothers, take this troublesome boy away from my sight. His tall tales are casting a cloud over our celebra—'

A great roar cut Bader off as a nearby hovel shattered to splinters and the troll prince Turv burst out through it!

Raf spun, his body tensing.

The troll prince gripped a great hammer in one fist. His fingerbone necklace hung askew around his neck, he was foaming at the mouth, and his eyes bore the fire of madness. Amid the chaos of the destruction of Troll Mountain, the troll prince had gone insane.

The tribesfolk scattered, fleeing into the shadows, hiding behind the hovels ringing the central square.

The chief, Bader, and their warrior kin all scurried fearfully behind the wooden throne.

Only one member of the tribe stood his ground.

Raf remained rooted to the spot in the centre of the village, beside the blazing fire, standing deathly still, eyeing the troll.

Turv bellowed with rage. 'I am here to wreak my vengeance on the one who stole our Elixir and destroyed our mountain! That kingdom was to be mine! *Mine!* Now it is nothing!'

At those words, Timbuk emerged timidly from his hiding place and called, 'The hero is here, dirty troll. He goes by the name of Bader!' Timbuk pointed at Bader. 'There he is and he will get the better of you again!'

The troll prince glanced at Bader and snorted derisively. 'When last I saw that one, he was skulking away from the fray like a snivelling toad.'

The troll feinted at Bader and Bader spun in fright to flee, only to trip on a rock, and he fell forward and the bottles of Elixir were smashed between his body and the ground. They shattered, sending the yellow fluid pooling in the dirt.

'No,' Turv said, turning slowly. 'The one I seek is . . .'

His eyes found Raf.

'. . . him. He is the one who destroyed my kingdom.'

Surprised murmurs rippled through the tribesfolk watching from the shadows.

Then the troll sprang at Raf and there in the centre of the village, surrounded by the members of the Northmen tribe, they fought.

It was a fast and terrible battle. The crazed troll swung his hammer wildly while Raf—weaponless—ducked and dived, using his speed to his advantage. No one in the tribe, not the warriors or anyone else, stepped forward to help him.

Then Turv lunged, overreaching, and Raf hurried past him, as he did so snatching something from the troll's weapons belt: his sharpened blade made of a human leg bone. Raf then quickly hurled himself sideways, diving *through* the fire, and rolled nimbly to his feet on the other side. Turv stomped around the fire in pursuit, his every footfall booming.

The big troll rounded the fire and suddenly Raf was in his face, driving forward with an outstretched hand, gripped in which was Turv's own bone-sword.

Raf drove the sharpened length of bone deep into the troll's left eye, thrusting it into his brain.

Turv froze in mid-stride. His hammer fell from his grip.

Then he dropped to his knees and froze for another moment . . . before he toppled forward and hit the ground face-first, forcing the bone-sword up through his head, its tip emerging from the back of his skull with a gruesome spurt of blood.

Then the troll prince lay still, dead, with Raf standing over him.

The village was silent.

The tribesfolk began to emerge from their hiding places, stepping out into the light, staring at Raf, at what he had just done.

Then they turned to gaze at Bader and the ruling family, still hiding behind the throne. Bader was staring at the shattered vials hanging from his neck strap, the precious yellow fluid now just a puddle in the dirt.

'Bader lied . . .' someone called. 'He lied to us!'

'Where is your courage now, Bader?' another spat.

Even Timbuk looked disbelievingly at Bader. 'It was all Raf's doing, not yours . . .' he said.

Raf just stared defiantly at the ruling family.

Then he addressed the tribesfolk in a tone he did not know he was capable of.

'I am leaving this valley and this tribe. Contrary to what we have been told, there are fertile plains beyond the mountains to the north and I plan to start a new tribe in those lands. I take with me knowledge of the disease: its cause *and* its cure. If you wish to stay with these "warriors", do so. I leave you in their care. But if you wish to join me, you may. I will leave at dawn and I will wait for no one.'

With those words, he turned and left the firelit area without so much as a backward glance, leaving the tribesfolk astounded, the head family mortified, and the corpse of the troll lying beside the crackling fire.

*

The following morning, nearly the whole tribe joined Raf as he left the valley forever. Among them was Timbuk. Only a handful of blood relations stayed behind with the former ruling family.

Raf's new tribe headed north, stopping briefly at the lemon grove near the river.

Raf ordered his followers to pick as many lemons as they could and to grind them into juice. That juice was then given to those affected by the disease, including Kira, and within days they showed signs of improvement. Their skin cleared and colour began to return to their gums.

On their way to their new home, Raf made one other stop: in the Badlands.

Leaving his new tribe, he ventured alone to Ko's shack in the swamp. It lay abandoned.

Raf left Ko a note:

DEAR KO,

I HAVE LEARNED MY FINAL LESSON AND LEARNED IT WELL.

I RECALLED YOUR WORDS: 'WHEN YOU GO IN SEARCH OF ELIXIRS, BE SURE YOU KNOW EXACTLY WHAT AN ELIXIR IS.'

NOW I KNOW.

AN ELIXIR IS NOT A MAGIC LIQUID. IT IS KNOWLEDGE. BOTTLES FILLED WITH MAGIC LIQUIDS EVENTUALLY RUN DRY, BUT KNOWLEDGE LASTS A LIFETIME.

YOU WILL BE PLEASED TO KNOW I HAVE USED MY NEWFOUND KNOWLEDGE TO MAKE MY SISTER AND MY TRIBE WELL AGAIN. WE HAVE LEFT OUR VALLEY IN SEARCH OF NEW LANDS TO THE NORTH.

BE WELL, KO, AND THANK YOU AGAIN FOR YOUR WISDOM.

YOUR FRIEND,

RAF

Raf left the shack and, with his new tribe following him, headed north.

He did not know that the whole time he had been at the shack, he had been watched from afar: by Ko and the wise troll, Vilnar.

Ko smiled as Raf left. He smiled even more broadly when he read the note.

He was never seen or heard from in those parts again. Where he and Vilnar went, no one knew.

*

Düm and Graia lived out their days in peace and tranquillity in a far corner of the Black Mountains.

*

The remnants of the Northmen tribe, which was really just the remainder of Bader's clan, all soon succumbed to the dreadful disease, dying out one by one, until none of them remained.

*

Raf and Kira found a new life in the plains to the north of the Black Mountains.

There Raf's tribe flourished under his leadership. He would lead them for many years, always urging the children to seek out new knowledge, to aspire to wisdom, and to question the old tales; well, all the tales except for one, the one which Raf himself told every year at harvest time, the story of his incredible adventure at Troll Mountain.

AN INTERVIEW WITH MATTHEW REILLY
ABOUT *TROLL MOUNTAIN*

Matthew, what inspired you to write *Troll Mountain*, a novel that is so different to your previous work?

I'm a guy who is interested in pretty much everything. I watch all kinds of movies, from blockbusters to obscure documentaries. I go to all sorts of cultural events: one week, I might go to an art show, the next I might see WrestleMania. I don't care if something is deemed high-brow or low-brow. I also listen to a lot of music, from modern pop to 1980s hits to the odd piece of classical music.

The idea for *Troll Mountain* came from listening to the very famous classical music piece 'In the Hall of the Mountain King' by Edvard Grieg. (Google it, you will know it. Trust me! Every third movie trailer uses it.) I was introduced to this wonderful piece of music when I was a teenager at school.

What few people know is that this piece of music was originally written in the late 1800s to accompany a play called *Peer Gynt* by Henrik Ibsen. In the play (as it was told to me) Peer Gynt dreams of being chased by a horde of trolls out of their underground kingdom as it collapses around them. I always thought this was a fantastic image—a lone guy fleeing from a great crowd of trolls—and, over the years, I wondered if I could craft a story around it.

Anyway, I recently had some spare time between novels and my mind returned to 'In the Hall of the Mountain King'. I found myself wondering: what would an entire *civilisation* of trolls look like . . . where would they live . . . and how could I get a young hero into their midst and have him flee from them as their kingdom crashes down around them?

As far as the first two questions were concerned, I would have my trolls live in a forbidding peak called Troll Mountain and their civilisation would be a brutish one based on the use of force.

As for the last question, I have always enjoyed heroes' journeys (like *Star Wars*, *The Lord of the Rings* and the *Harry Potter* series), so I decided that I would write a pure hero's journey story: a lone youth would venture out of his familiar world into the dark and scary world of the trolls.

Why release it online first, before this print edition?

I guess I'm just always looking for new ways to reach out to readers.

Many of you will recall that *Hover Car Racer* was originally released online in serialised parts. That was back in 2004. Now, looking back, I think it was a little ahead of its time. The Internet and e-books were not mature enough then for such a release. Now, however, I think it's different. E-books and e-readers are now widespread and big-screen smartphones from companies like Apple and Samsung make reading an online story very easy.

I like the idea of someone sitting on a bus, train or subway being able to download and read a fun shorter story on the way home from work. Or a school librarian being able to read it aloud in class.

I'm not sure this would work as well with a full-length novel, but with a novel like *Troll Mountain*, I think it works very well.

***Troll Mountain* is a very family-friendly story. Is there a reason for this?**

I see *Troll Mountain* as an action-fable that the whole family can enjoy. Through the vehicle of a (hopefully) entertaining action-packed quest, for me, it's about questioning those in authority, social hierarchies, and conventional wisdom. This is something that I think all people, but especially young people, should do in their everyday lives.

You've really written some varied stories in recent years: *Scarecrow and the Army of Thieves*, *The Tournament*, *The Great Zoo of China* and *Troll Mountain*. Is there a reason for this?

I can understand why some of my readers would be feeling confused lately! After all, I have bounced from the high-octane energy and considerable violence of *Scarecrow and the Army of Thieves* to the very adult themes in *The Tournament* to *The Great Zoo of China* that is a pedal-to-the-metal thriller that takes action to a whole new level, and the fantasy-fable of *Troll Mountain*.

Honestly, I don't set out to confuse anyone. I just write the story that interests me at a given time. Maybe I was in a darker place when I wrote *The Tournament*—who knows? Maybe I was in a lighter mood when I wrote *Troll Mountain*—that might be the case.

As an author, as the years pass, you grow and, like it or not, you change. My readers have always been very generous in allowing me to try new things with my books—moving from Scarecrow to Jack West, or trying the odd stand-alone novel like

Hover Car Racer (which could conceivably also be called something of a fable), *The Tournament* or *The Great Zoo of China*.

In fact, *The Tournament* is a good example of me growing as an author. It was not a book I could have written in my twenties. As a tale about the relationship between a teacher and a student, it was a story that I grew into writing.

I hope my readers will always know that, no matter what the subject, every story with my name on it will always—*always*—have the 'Matthew Reilly engine' powering it along, and that means it'll be fast and entertaining, even if it's about a chess tournament in 1546!

Troll Mountain makes some pointed observations about how societies operate. Can you take us through what motivated you to write about that?

For me, a good fable should have a positive central theme, something that guides us in our lives. As I see it, the main theme of *Troll Mountain* is: education should always trump brute force.

Raf succeeds because he learns. He learns that it's better to know *how to make* an elixir than simply to find one.

An extension of this—for me, anyway—is the story's analysis of societal structures. Many readers will notice the similarities between Raf's tribal structure and that of the troll civilisation, in particular, how they are both ruled by the thugs and bullies of their respective social groups. This was very deliberate.

It came from my observations of the world today. If you look at our world as you watch the evening news, you will see that, even now in the early 21st century, there are essentially two types of societies: those in which everyone's talent is harnessed and where physical strength is not the sole determinant of status; and those where guys with guns rule (i.e. military regimes).

The greatest leap forward a society can make, in my humble opinion, is when that society's army pledges to obey its parliament under all circumstances. Societies ruled by thugs and military regimes will, by virtue of their very nature, stagnate and eventually die. Guys with guns do not innovate, nor do they inspire any innovation from those they rule over by force. Whereas if we let talented people do their thing—work in politics, science, engineering, or the arts—society will flourish and we will fly to the moon and back. One of the richest men in the world today, Bill Gates, wears glasses and is of modest build. In a society ruled by thugs and brute force, he would never have succeeded. Smarts should always trump brute strength.

Tell us about Bader, the human villain of the story. He is certainly a character you love to hate.

For me, a secondary theme of the book is how Raf learns about human nature and people's motivations. Sadly, not everyone in this world works for the greater good and we all must discover this at some point in our lives. (I reckon it's better to learn this in a book than for real!)

I very much enjoyed creating Bader. He is, quite simply, a young man who is totally and utterly selfish. Hopefully the part near the end of the story—where he steals the Elixir from the true hero, Raf, and returns as a hero to the tribe—grates with readers.

This is because Bader's heroic status is unearned. We have watched Raf toil and struggle for days and days, and suddenly there's Bader, who is entirely unworthy, claiming all the credit! I'm a big fan of comeuppance in a story and Bader's comeuppance was one of my favourite scenes to write. Raf needs an external witness to verify that Bader was actually a coward and he gets it from the most unlikely source, the troll prince, Turv.

Oh, and by the way, for those who are interested and who didn't already figure it out, the illness that afflicts the tribe and the trolls (and its cure) bears a striking resemblance to scurvy.

What does the future hold?

It's been a busy time and now I think it's time to rest and recharge. I'd like to make the next few years really special, storywise, and that means choosing the best story to write. Having written such varied stuff over the last few years, I find myself with lots of sequel options: a new Jack West, or perhaps a sequel to *The Tournament*, or even a follow-up to *Great Zoo*. But then, I enjoy creating new heroes as well. As always, I'll go with the story that most excites me, because in the end, it's the excitement that I inject in the writing-stage that leaps off the page when readers read the book.

Any final words?

The same ones I always finish with: I just hope you enjoyed the book.

Matthew Reilly
Sydney, Australia
June 2015

MORE BESTSELLING TITLES FROM MATTHEW REILLY

Hover Car Racer

Meet Jason Chaser, hover car racer. He's won himself a place at the International Race School, where racers either make it on to the Pro Circuit – or they crash and burn.

But he's an outsider. He's younger than the other racers. His car, the *Argonaut*, is older. And on top of that, someone doesn't want him to succeed at the School and will do anything to stop him.

Now Jason Chaser isn't just fighting for his place on the starting line, he's racing for his life.

MORE BESTSELLING TITLES FROM
MATTHEW REILLY

Hover Car Racer

Meet Jason Chaser, hover car racer. He's won a chance to prove himself at the International Race School, where some of the world's best young drivers learn to drive, to race, to crash and burn.

But he's an outsider. He's younger than the other racers. He has the best car — but that, and on top of that, someone doesn't want him to succeed at the school and will do anything to stop him.

Now Jason Chaser has time to think about how he got to the starting line. He's racing for his life...

Contest

The New York State Library. A brooding labyrinth
of towering bookcases, narrow aisles and spiralling
staircases. For Doctor Stephen Swain and his
daughter, Holly, it is the site of a nightmare. For one
night, this historic building is to be the venue for a
contest. A contest in which Swain is to compete –
whether he likes it or not.

The rules are simple. Seven contestants will enter.
Only one will leave. With his daughter in his arms,
Swain is plunged into a terrifying fight for survival.
He can choose to run, to hide or to fight – but if
he wants to live, he has to win. For in this contest,
unless you leave as the victor, you do not leave at all.